# BATTLE
# EARTH V

NICK S. THOMAS

First published in the United Kingdom in Feb 2012 by Swordworks Books.

ISBN 978-1-909149-06-9

Typeset by Swordworks Books
Printed and bound in the UK & US
A catalogue record of this book is available
from the British Library

Cover design by Swordworks Books
www.swordworks.co.uk

# BATTLE
# EARTH V

NICK S. THOMAS

# PROLOGUE

Alien forces had taken Mars, occupied and defeated the Moon forces, but they could not defeat Earth. A bloody year long war had driven them off the planet and Earth forces had been quick to re-take the Moon and all that was theirs.

The alien threat was gone. The only known living creatures were signed up soldiers in Colonel Chandra's Inter-Allied Battalion. Tartaros, the enemy mother ship, had seemingly vanished from the solar system. Peace had returned.

Despite the relief of the humans, the knowledge that a fearful enemy still loomed out there in the depths of space weighed heavily on all their hearts. There was not one among the population of Earth that did not want to believe the war was over.

Could it really be true?

# CHAPTER ONE

"Come, move!"

Troops rushed past Colonel Chandra with sweat pouring down their uniforms. Summer was fast approaching, and the horrors of war seemed a distant memory. The narrow footbridge she was stood on shook violently as the remainder of her Battalion trundled onwards.

"Move it! Move it!" she shouted.

Jones approached at the head of his Company and stopped to take a breather as he gestured for the others to continue. He could see she was as sweat covered and exhausted as the rest of them, and yet she persisted and did everything to show no sign of fatigue.

"The heat too much for you, Captain?" she asked.

"Damn right. Don't you think we've all had enough for one day? They've all been waiting for the war to be over for so long, yet here we still are at the grindstone."

"This is our job, remember. We can't afford to go slack just because we have seen success. Follow me."

Jones sighed from both his exhaustion and the Colonel's seemingly unending energy. They tacked on to the side of his Company and followed on several hundred metres to the end of the course. At the end of the route, they found hundreds of weary faces and troops panting to get their breath. The last few of the half strength Battalion were making their way in.

"Everyone listen up!"

Several of the troops who had sat down staggered to their feet. Within a few seconds, all had arrived and stood in silence in a circle around Chandra. At her feet were several Assegais, the close combat tool that Reiter has provided. Jones shook his head in disbelief, as he could already see what was coming.

"The last war taught us that we must be prepared and able to fight at all distances. The ability to effectively wield the Assegai is something we are all new to, but we must master it quickly!"

Blinker yawned loudly as she finished.

"Am I keeping you up, Private?"

Monty stood beside him and smirked at the grilling his brother was about to receive.

"Step forward, Private. You too, Corporal!"

The two of them sighed but obliged.

They wore full packs and had to carry their Reiter rifles

without the exoskeleton suits the scientist had developed. Chandra was eager to keep them fit and healthy. They wore their old body armour. It wasn't enough to withstand an energy pulse, but it sure worked well to weigh them down during their run.

"Put down your rifles!" she ordered.

She picked up two of the Assegais and tossed them over to the brothers.

"I had these put together for future training; same weight and feel of the real thing, but they just put out a small charge, which you'll be sure to know if you've been hit. This is effectively an MPs stone baton."

"Great," muttered Blinker.

The Colonel ignored his rambling, knowing she'd teach him a lesson soon enough.

"Remember, you can strike humans with the edge and break jaws, crush skulls and break limbs, but not against an armoured Krycenaean. The thrust is the only way you can hope to hurt them. They are bigger, stronger and better armoured than we can hope to be. Our strength is in our agility and our speed. If you blunder about like an ox, you will die."

She lifted one of the training Assegais and pointed at the two brothers to pick them up. They looked surprised, as she was gesturing for them both to come at her.

"What's wrong? Don't want the opportunity to strike an officer? Or are you not up to the task?"

A reserved and quiet laughter broke out amongst those watching and in that moment, the two brothers felt their anger grow. None of them liked being humiliated before the unit. They'd never heard the Colonel be so confrontational. They snatched up the weapons and rushed at her.

Blinker was ahead of his brother, and in his rage, swung a wide horizontal swing just as the Colonel had told him not to. She nimbly ducked and rolled under it. She landed firmly back on her feet and thrust her Assegai into Monty's hip, a little below his armour. She'd rolled forward so quickly against their charge that he'd not even got his weapon forward before he felt the electrical charge pulse through his body.

The Corporal shook violently before going limp and dropping to the ground. She had not seen their effect before and smiled at the result. Chandra quickly straightened her legs and turned to face Blinker who had turned from his bullish charge and was coming back at her.

It was clear he had learnt something from his previous mistake and thrust forward as he rushed. Chandra tilted her body just enough to allow the weapon to pass over her right shoulder as she drove her knee into his groin. The Private keeled over her hip and winced in pain. She pushed him back, striking him with a hard left hook that smashed him to the ground.

The audience remained silent as they looked on at the

two veteran soldiers lying incapacitated, and the Colonel not having a scratch. Their smiles were gone. She could already tell the lesson was getting through.

"I don't mind you hating our enemy. Despise them, but never let your rage and anger drive you to recklessness. You are all professional soldiers. Our training is preparation for the real thing, and you must treat it as such!"

She paced around the arena her audience had created. She was pleased with herself but equally disappointed in her opponents.

"I know you're tired. I know I've worked you hard. But let us not forget the conditions we had to fight in. We often went into combat with minimal sleep, exhausted and hungry. If you cannot fight to the best of your ability in such conditions, then you are not fit to be in this Battalion!"

Jones sighed but nodded in agreement at the same time. It was a lesson hard learned. They were being pushed to the limits of their bodies, but he knew she was right to do it.

"Today's training is over. Rest and relax for the rest of the day, but remember today. Tomorrow we start hand-to-hand training from the start. Well done to you all for making it here and in good time. I am at least glad to see that fitness levels are being maintained. That'll be all, fallout."

\* \* \*

Taylor's eyes opened softly to see the comforts of his officer's quarters in Camp Pendleton where he'd been back for only two days. The bed was soft and comfortable, the air fresh, and the temperature perfect. Beside him, he could feel Eli nestled into his side. It was a life of luxury he'd almost grown to forget. She stirred from a deep sleep and stretched out. Eli looked around for a moment as if surprised by her surroundings. Then she turned to Taylor and smiled at the realisation it was all real.

"I'll never get bored of this," she whispered.

Taylor smiled in agreement.

"Where do you think Jones and the Colonel are now? We've been with them so long, its weird to be apart."

"Well I guess Jones will be catching up with his wife. She won't be too happy to not have seen him for a year."

"He's married?" she responded in surprise.

"Jones is an Englishman. He'd never discuss her publically. I only found out a few months back. Chandra is probably busting someone's balls and preparing for the next battle."

"Really? You don't think she's kicking back for a bit?"

He turned and looked to see if she was being serious before nodding with a smile.

"No way."

He looked at his watch and sighed.

"We gotta go."

"Ah, come on," she pleaded.

"Hey, we're living like kings compared to what we had to put up with, so let's appreciate what we have. We're still marines, remember that."

She sighed. She knew he was right, but getting out of bed in that moment seemed like the least logical action in the world to both of them. Eli groaned once again as she sat up and reached for her shirt. She stopped for a moment, looking at Taylor.

"Inter-Allied, what will happen to it now?" she asked.

"What do you mean?"

"The war is over. We're divided by the Atlantic and of different nations, and we have no headquarters or official status."

"The war may be over, but it won't be the last. One thing this has taught the world, is that our armies need to work more closely with each other. Inter-Allied will continue on. Don't you worry about that."

"It's hard to imagine how it can work any longer. Separated like this, how can we continue the way we were?"

"That's something to discuss over the coming weeks. For now, I think everyone is just happy to be back home and enjoying a little peace. Or what little peace the Colonel will allow our British friends. Come on, our two Companies will be forming up as I ordered. We can't be late."

"You're in charge around here now, and you can be whatever you want to be," she said with a smile.

She was clearly touting for more time in bed, and it was

an alluring proposition, but he couldn't allow himself to give in, no matter how tempting.

"Whilst we remain in the Corps, we'll act like marines, Sergeant."

She smiled in response at the hilarity of the comment, considering their current situation.

"Hey, I'm not saying a few rules can't be bent here and there, but we can never let it get in the way of our duties."

She nodded in agreement.

Ten minutes later, they were out on the parade ground, where Silva had formed up the two Companies Taylor currently commanded. Jackson and Ota were stood chatting until he came in to view. They quickly turned as Silva called the rest of the other ranks to attention. Taylor nodded in greeting and thanks to the Sergeant Major as he came to a halt, taking a deep breath and surveyed the troops before him. Only a few months ago he knew few of their names, and now they were tightly knit comrades.

They were still missing a number from those killed or wounded in combat, but they were at better strength than almost any time during the war.

"Stand easy!"

Mitch was glad to see the relief in their faces that they were once again on home soil and without the ever-imposing danger of the enemy. At the end of Jackson's Company, the two alien allies stood in formation, mimicking everything the others did. They were still not bound to any platoon or company. All that was certain; they were with Taylor, and they would remain with Inter-Allied. The towering creatures shadowed the men alongside them.

It struck Mitch that none among the Inter-Allied looked upon the two aliens with any doubt or fear any longer. There was no hiding the fact they were different, but they had been accepted within the unit. Like the others, they wore no armour that morning. Their skin-tight body suits had been sprayed in a camouflage pattern that resembled the fabric the rest of them wore, and their sleeves were emblazoned with the same insignia.

On their right arms they wore large Star and Stripes. It was an odd sight to see, but they all knew it was necessary to keep them from being shot by friendly forces.

"Good morning to you all! And what a morning it is!"

He looked up at the gleaming sky, squinting at the low sun that was already promising a blisteringly hot day.

"During the war, you received no leave, no rest, no R&R. Our orders are to re-equip and re-assemble to be back on our feet at full combat effectiveness within three weeks. I am sorry I cannot let you take the time we all deserve, but we cannot risk weeks to pass, without getting back on top of things."

The grimaces of disappointment were hard to conceal. He smiled in response and continued on.

"However, as acting commander of the Battalion on this base, I am issuing you all three days leave."

Cheers rang out as the troops could barely contain themselves.

"Pipe down!" Silva's booming voice barrelled around the parade ground, quickly bringing them under control.

"I'll see you all back here Monday morning, 0600 hours. Until then, your time is your own! Inter-Allied, fallout!"

The cheers and laughter broke out once again as the troops scattered quickly, to find loved ones and any enjoyment they could. Taylor smiled as he watched their sheer joy, but he stopped as he noticed Jafar and Tsengal still stood at ease. Parker leapt to his side in joy, but he brushed her off.

"Hang on a minute."

He walked over to the two aliens still stood, awaiting their orders.

"I appreciate this brings us to a difficult position. You joined us as soldiers, but there is now not a war to fight."

"There is always another war on the horizon," replied Jafar.

Taylor smiled. He wasn't sure whether to feel comfort in their support, or sadness in that they were probably right.

"You've got free movement around this base. Just be sure to be in uniform at all times, and to keep your ID cards handy. We are proud to have you among us. You earned our trust and respect, but it will not come so quickly to the rest of this world."

"Thank you," replied Jafar.

Taylor was taken aback by their response, as if they should be thankful for what little faith was placed in them.

"I cannot promise you will be treated fairly by many humans. You must remember the horrors we faced against your kind. There is little you can do that will help them overcome it. They need time. Continue to do what you're doing, and eventually you'll, well, fit in."

"Lieutenant Rains suggested he could use our help," stated Tsengal.

Taylor turned in curiosity but had no answer where there was not a question.

"May we assist him?"

Taylor nodded. "Of course, I'm sure he could use a hand. Crazy bastard would rather work on his bird than take a little time out."

"A true warrior," replied Jafar.

"Maybe, or maybe he just has a screw loose."

The two creatures looked confused by his statement and went silent.

"I'm out of here. Remember what I said. Stick to base, keep insignia on at all times, avoid restricted areas, and you'll be just fine. I'll see you Monday morning."

Mitch turned and grabbed Parker. She giggled as he tore her away to the jeep they had waiting.

"Where we heading, Sir?" she jested.

"When was the last time you kicked back on a beach,

Sergeant?"

She smiled in response. Half an hour later they were at San Onofre, laying in front a beach hut they'd not seen since long before the war had begun. They knew that come the evening it would be a hive of activity, but until the end of the working day, they could enjoy the peace. Time seemed to pass them by as they relaxed and slowly fell into a deep sleep.

The constant bleep of Taylor's communicator caused him to spring up. He hit the answer button and responded in a croaky voice.

"Taylor."

"Mitch, you want to get your ass over here now. MPs are here with a particularly abrasive son of a bitch. They are trying to arrest our two alien friends."

"What? Why?" he asked.

"Nothing they have done. Apparently, they're acting like they are hunting for spies."

"Christ, Eddie, where are Jafar and Tsengal now?"

"I hid them in a maintenance room, but they'll not last long there. I sent the MPs packing, but they'll soon be back when they find out the two of them were supposed to be here."

"Alright, you just hold on. Do not let any bastard touch two of our own!"

"You got it, but you hurry on up here now. I can't fight them off alone."

Taylor leapt to his feet, which caused Eli to rouse and sit up with a smile. She looked disgruntled and disappointed that he was in such a flurry during their only leave in over a year. Then she noticed the concern in his face and quickly rubbed her eyes and tried to come to.

"What is it?"

"Jafar and Tsengal, MPs are trying to arrest them!"

She sighed, and he already knew she was put out by his support of the creatures. She shook her head in disapproval, but that only served to anger Mitch.

"Those two are part of us. Would you leave any other one of the Company in such a time?"

"No, but they aren't one of us, are they?"

"People have said the same about female soldiers and black soldiers not so long ago. They stand with us, and that's enough for me."

"For Christ's sake, will we never get a break?" she complained.

"Do what you like, but I'll not leave them behind."

He pulled on his shirt and buttoned it quickly as he rushed to the vehicle. Eli watched him leap aboard in a furious manner, speeding away from the tranquil paradise she had so recently been enjoying.

"You fool," she whispered.

Taylor was already travelling well over the speed limit by the time he passed the gates to the road, and dust and sand swept in through the open sides of the jeep. His shirt was only half buttoned, and he was still wearing sandals. It was far from the well-kept image he maintained on base, but there was no time to change.

"God damn fucking bastards," he yelled to himself as he hit the wheel of the car.

"I go for two God damn minutes, and they try to fuck us in the ass."

Taylor had no love of the MPs, few did, but he genuinely had more than enough reasons to want to shoot some of them. Many despised him because of his combat record and all the glory they felt it brought. It was an envy he had to deal with on a regular basis.

Mitch could feel his head pounding as his anger and rage built. He reached the base gates in half the time it had taken the two of them to get to the beach. The dusty jeep came to a halt at the guard post, and a Corporal stepped forward to check his ID. The man looked suspicious of Taylor's rough appearance, as he rightfully should be.

The Corporal desperately wanted to say something about his ill disciplined attire but looked to the rank on his shoulders, and knew he could not risk insult if Taylor really was what he was claiming.

"Identification, Sir?"

"For Christ's sake," he muttered.

Taylor reached into his pocket and fumbled around for his card that had seen so little use. He'd long forgotten what life was like at home.

"Here," he snapped, passing the man a bent identify card. It was heavily worn and slightly burnt in one corner. The guard looked in shock at the card and took it suspiciously from his hands. Taylor sat impatiently.

"Well, come on, I haven't got all day," insisted Taylor.

"Uhh, yes, Sir."

The man lifted his scanner, twisting the bent card to make it read properly and stood surprised as Mitch's name and identity was displayed. There wasn't a marine on base that didn't know the name.

"Major Taylor, sorry for the delay, Sir."

Mitch snatched the card from the Corporal's hands and put his foot to the floor. The jeep raced forward and narrowly made it through the gates. They were only half open when he squeezed through. The Corporal shook his head in astonishment.

"Crazy bastard."

Taylor's jeep slid around the first corner, and he was quickly able to open up the throttle and tear across an open road towards Rains' hangar. He slammed the brakes on and slid to a halt at the open doors where the pilot sat with his feet up as if it were any other day.

"Where are they, Eddie?"

The Lieutenant took another sip from his mug, not affected at all by the Major's flustered state. He sighed and turned to Taylor, signalling over his shoulder with his eyes and a nod. Taylor turned to see three military police vehicles approaching. He snapped back around.

"We can't keep them hidden forever," mused Eddie.

Taylor shook his head. He knew his old friend was right, but it weighed heavily on his conscience that he would have to give up his own men, without them committing an offence. He turned back and stood confidently upright, glaring at the approaching vehicles. His right hand instinctively reached down to his thigh to rest on the pistol that had lived there for the last year, but it was nowhere to be found. He looked down in shock at the realisation that he was unarmed.

*Caught without a weapon, for God's sake,* he thought.

The recent peace had let Mitch slip back into an easy life, not yet earned. He coughed to clear his throat and prepare himself for the assault of the MPs. The three jeeps slid to an abrupt halt less than ten metres from his position, and eight soldiers leapt from them. At least they were officially soldiers; Taylor could never see them as such.

"I am Captain Ames. We are looking for the two aliens under your command, Major."

Taylor grimaced. He had hoped they were unaware of who he was. He quickly realised that they were well informed, and he was not going to talk his way out of it.

"On what charge do you wish to arrest men under my command?"

The Captain squinted in surprise at Mitch's description of the creatures.

"The alien soldiers known as Jafar and Tsengal are soldiers of an enemy army which sought to conquer this world. The reason for their arrest should not need explanation."

Taylor's face turned to bitter anger.

"I do not need reminding what this war was about. I fought it whilst you lay about polishing your pretty uniforms. I will not surrender any under my command without just cause."

Before the Captain could respond a door opened behind Eddie, and they all stopped to look. The two alien soldiers step out from hiding. The MPs quickly lifted their handguns.

"Whoa!" yelled Taylor. Tell your men to stand down!"

He looked back to see the two creatures stepping slowly towards the group, without showing any signs of aggression. Taylor snapped back around and roared at the troops.

"Put your weapons down!"

The Captain lifted his hand and signalled them to lower their pistols, in an attempt to alleviate the situation. The two stopped before Taylor, and Jafar finally spoke.

"We will do as is ordered. We will not hide from this any longer."

"No, they can't do this!"

He turned back around. "Who gave these orders?"

"I do not have that information, Sir. We are only doing

our job. They are happy to surrender, so let us get this done, and there need not be any further trouble."

The Captain stepped forward to pass right through the Major without stopping. Taylor could see he was uneasy with the task he had been given, but nothing was going to convince him to act against those orders. Mitch reached forward, firmly grasping the hand in which the MP carried his pistol and twisted until the man yelped in pain. Taylor struck him on the nose with one firm knife hand blow that caused his nose to burst and throw blood over his gleaming uniform.

Two more of the MPs rushed forward with batons in one hand and pistols in the other. One took a swing for him, and he nimbly ducked under the clumsy and excessive swing. He thrust an uppercut into the man's stomach, throwing him off his feet, and quickly turned to the other. The baton was thrust forward at him with a more experienced fighter than the last. He narrowly avoided it with a quick sidestep. Before the MP could respond, he wrapped his one arm around the elbow and pushed with his other hand. The man's arm snapped in on itself, driving the shock baton into his chest.

The MP spasmed from the voltage pulsing through his body, and he collapsed with the loss of motor control. Taylor looked up to see that remainder of the MPs were lifting their pistols to fire, but he was too far away to do much about it. He defiantly stood over his vanquished foes, praying they would not shoot a superior officer.

Taylor's face grew long as he saw the look in their eyes. They were willing to pull the trigger, and he could do nothing but hope for a miracle. Two shots rang out, but as they did so, Jafar leapt in front of the Major. The small calibre rounds ricocheted from his armour and hit the hangar beside them.

The alien dwarfed Taylor and completely blocked the MPs view of him. Jafar stood calmly between them. He had no weapon in hand nor made any attempt to join in the fight. Taylor stepped around his newly found friend to see the two MPs stood in shock. He could see just a tiny bit of the horror he had first witnessed on the beaches in France upon their first meet with the enemy.

The MPs still held their weapons high and trained on the alien, but they knew that any more shots would be futile. They stood silently, awaiting the next move. Taylor turned to Jafar and looked at him in surprise. It was in part for saving his life once more, but more from the restraint he had shown in not fighting back.

"These men come to take you away. I cannot say for certain their reasons, but I can say that it will not be pleasant. They want you for lab rats."

Jafar shrugged his shoulders.

"We both knew this day would come. Your commanders must have many questions for us, and we will assist them in any way we can."

"But not like this, you are with us now."

"And I follow your orders, just as you must follow your superiors. Do not throw your life away so quickly."

The deep voice pierced Taylor's thoughts, and he instantly calmed himself.

"You never cease to amaze me. How on Earth can the rest of your race be the way they are, when you bare so little resemblance?"

"Just one of the questions which will require an answer in the coming days."

The area went silent as all reflected on what had just happened. The MPs on the ground reeled in sighs of pain. Then the silence was broken by the rushed pace of a jeep soaring towards the hangar bay. The vehicle bore the stars of General White. It slid to a halt, and Sergeant Gibbons leapt out, the General's driver. He had two marines with him. Neither were MPs.

Gibbons stopped and quickly surveyed the scene, shaking his head at the bloodied police on the ground.

"Christ, Major, the war's over, and yet you want to keep fighting?"

Had it been any other Sergeant questioning him, he would have been most put out, but Gibbons commanded respect across the base.

"I didn't come looking for one. These idiots came to arrest troops under my command, without right or reason."

"The two aliens are being brought in for questioning by direct orders of General White, and even if you can get away with this incident, you will not defy the General and get away with it."

Taylor suddenly felt the tension in his body release, and his pulse calm at the sobering realisation of what a mess he had made. He was still bitterly angry about what was about to happen, but now knew he could not stop it.

"I want to speak with the General immediately!"

"And he is waiting for you. In the meantime, you will step aside and allow the MPs to carry out their orders."

He thought about it for a moment, finally nodding in agreement. The MPs lowered their weapons and went to the aid of the others. Mitch stepped forward and reached out his arm to help one to his feet.

"Please understand I was only protecting my own. I meant you no harm."

The man nodded as he gritted his teeth.

"Not much of an apology," he replied.

"A fitting one, considering your actions."

The man scowled, but Gibbons immediately cut in.

"That's enough, gentlemen! This situation has already been messy enough. Major Taylor, please join me."

He gestured for Taylor to follow him. Mitch looked back for a moment to Eddie who stood with a rifle in hand. He had no doubt the Lieutenant would have been willing to use it had the fight escalated. He nodded in gratitude before turning and continuing on to the jeep.

*It's gonna be a long fucking day,* he thought.

# CHAPTER TWO

Taylor stood to attention before the General's desk. White ignored him and continued to read through information on a datapad. The door opened once again, and another soldier stepped into the room. Taylor turned slightly and saw it was Captain Ames. He held a blood soaked cloth to his nose that was still gushing. The blood was smeared over his cheeks, and it had already dried to a flat brown over the white straps of his MPs webbing. General White looked up at the injured man and turned sternly to Taylor.

"This is Captain Ames, a military police officer who you struck whilst he was carrying out his orders. I know you have no love of MPs, Major, but when you undermine them, you undermine me."

Taylor butted in, despite it being completely unacceptable for him to do so.

"On what orders were they arresting honest and reliable

soldiers? Last I looked, we protected our own, simper fi, Sir!"

White's face began to redden with rage, but he quickly calmed himself before he responded.

"Major, we have a lot to learn about their race. We must do everything in our power to better prepare ourselves for the next potential war. I am sorry for the way this was handled, which was certainly clumsy and ill conceived, but that does not change the fact it was necessary."

"They are more than happy to help in any way, so why on Earth arrest them?"

"I find your trust in these aliens curious, Major, when you've probably been single-handedly responsible for more of their deaths than any other human being."

Taylor tried to butt in, but White didn't let him.

"They are aliens, aliens! They may indeed have defected, but I'd like to know for certain. And if they truly are on our side, then they can fill in many blanks."

Taylor shook his head.

"I agree they can do that, but sending this idiot to imprison them was a dumbass move. We're only lucky Jafar and Tsengal saw reason. They had every right to tear Ames and his MPs apart."

Ames gasped and tried to speak up, but White interrupted.

"Captain, you've caused enough trouble today. I have no doubt your CO will have much to say about it. You can tell him from me that he'll suffer if he pursues this."

Ames begrudgingly nodded in agreement.

"Now get out and get that looked at!"

Taylor smiled at the MP being sent packing with his tail between his legs. The door slammed behind him, and Mitch looked back to see White with his head in his hands.

"Jesus, Mitch, can you never stay out of trouble?" he whispered.

Taylor didn't respond. He knew the General was as in as much a difficult spot as himself.

"I put out an order for the two aliens to be brought in for questioning. I did not ask for them to be arrested, nor treated as the enemy. If you honestly believe they are on our side and willing to bet your life on it, which you clearly are, then I believe you're right."

"Thank you, Sir."

"Now, these creatures are not human, and therefore are not necessarily bound by our law, unless we choose to treat them as enemy combatants. For now, they will remain in holding for their own protection and to assist us in our research. As a result, you may visit them anytime you like. You, as their acting CO may be present during any and all questioning that takes places, and I suggest you are."

"It just seems wrong, Sir. These two have proven themselves to us more than a few times already. They are as much marines as you and I. They deserve better."

"I never said it was fair, Mitch. We need information.

We cannot fret about upsetting a few individuals as a result of that. You above all should understand that."

Taylor nodded in agreement.

"Got it, Sir."

"And for God's sake, stop getting into fights. I can only get you out of so much shit. The only reason you have got away with it all so far is based on your war record. The further we get from your glory days, the less leeway you'll get."

"Those MPs are total assholes, Sir. When will the day come when we don't have to put up with such shit?"

"When you die or retire."

Taylor smiled as he turned and walked to the door.

"The questioning of your two friends is being undertaken by Major Weller. He has strict orders to inform you before any and all contact."

"Thank you, Sir."

He stepped out of the room and looked down to see a few specs of blood on the floor where Ames had rushed off. The thought brought a smile to his face, and he quickly set off to find his two imprisoned friends.

* * *

Jones stepped into the officers' mess and was immediately greeted pleasantly by many that knew of his reputation. He passed through them and exchanged a few greetings, as he made his way to the bar where he hoped to find Chandra. She was sat alone there, exactly as he had expected. She was savouring a whiskey that had clearly been stood for a while. She was never one to drink to excess, but he could tell she was far from at ease.

As he approached, she turned and acknowledged him but said nothing. He took a seat and asked for a drink. He looked once more and could see she was not ready to start a conversation.

"You don't exactly seem ecstatic to be home. Isn't this what we've been fighting for all this time?"

She took a small sip from her drink before answering him. Her voice was croaky. He didn't know whether it was as a result of sitting in silence for a few hours, or for shouting for most of the day.

"Everyone is slacking off, as if they can return to the easy lives they had before the war."

"Haven't we all earned that?"

"In theory, yes. But the war should have taught us a valuable lesson. That we weren't ready."

"How could we be?"

"You prepare for the next war, not the previous one."

"But we could never have had an idea of what was to come."

"True, but now we do."

Jones sighed. "I am not sure whether you want war or peace."

"Don't be ridiculous. I'd never want war, but that should not be a reason not to be ready for it."

"Do you know something I don't?"

She turned and smiled with a smug but friendly expression.

"Many things."

Her face turned serious once again.

"Commander Phillips tells me that we have intel of enemy positions not far from the Mars colony. He is in talks to get an operation launched to investigate."

"Mars? Not again?"

"Keep your voice down," she whispered.

He looked around to see if anyone else had noticed his shock, but they were too busy enjoying their drinks and conversation. She continued.

"Not an attacking force from what we can see. Phillips believes they have been there from the very start. Perhaps some kind of logistical troops."

"You don't sound convinced."

"It was our point of contact. They have maintained a presence throughout, and we still don't know how they reached our solar system."

"What do you mean?"

"Where do they come from, do you think? They cannot have originated in our solar system, or we'd have crossed paths long ago. It begs the question, how they got here? Their ships are fast, but it would take hundreds or thousands of years to reach a habitable planet, or wherever they came from."

"And you think whatever they have left here will give us the answers?"

She nodded.

"I know you're enjoying this new found peace, but it would be foolish and short sighted to forget what dangers still loom over us."

Jones turned and sat back against the bar. He panned across the room and took in the atmosphere. There was a level of excitement and comfort amongst all there he had not seen before. Surviving the war had given them all a new perspective on their lives. And yet, here he was, having his hopes and dreams shot down by the Colonel.

"You're going to volunteer for this investigative mission, aren't you?" he asked.

She didn't answer, but he knew what it meant.

"This why you're pushing the troops so hard?"

"I'm keeping them in shape and ready to fight because that is what is needed of them. If we go on this mission, it should come as no surprise."

"Can't we let someone else do the dirty work for once? Seems no matter where we are, we always get the shit."

"Plenty of soldiers had it hard in the war, just as hard as we did."

"I doubt that," he muttered.

She said nothing, and they both knew the world had

suffered during the war, but it was hard to think of anything worse than their own experiences.

"After all that they did to you, don't you want to take it to them?" she asked.

Jones twitched at the reminder of his experiences but peered into her eyes in surprise.

"Where does this bitterness come from?"

She didn't respond, as they both knew no good could come of it.

"We're going to Mars, the only question is when? Few will volunteer for it, so I can guarantee we'll be involved."

Jones stared at her for a moment. He wondered what she even wanted in life anymore. She seemed to live to fight.

*Is this what we have become?* He asked himself.

* * *

Taylor stepped into the holding cells where his two friends were being kept. Despite the General's speech about them assisting the allies in questioning, it still looked as much as a prison as it always had. Every time he saw the bars of a cell, or the guards around them, it left a foul taste in his mouth. He forever linked his incarceration with the far more horrific and mortifying ordeal Jones had endured. He could tell that most of the guards knew of his reputation and were watching him with both a careful and untrustworthy eye.

*Good, let them fear me.*

He was led to the cell at the end of the corridor, but there were no bars, they had been covered over with a one-way thick glass. He could see the two of them talking to each other, but the sound was completely deadened by the walls of the cell. Then the silence was broken by footsteps approaching; the walk of a confident and arrogant man. He already knew it would be their interrogator.

"Major Taylor, I presume?"

Mitch turned to see that the man was clearly well aware of who he was, but didn't want to admit it and risk stroking Taylor's ego. Mitch nodded. He saw no need to open his mouth just yet.

"I am Major Weller, Corps of Offworld Intelligence and Research."

"That's a mouthful," Taylor said quietly.

Weller smiled and tapped Taylor on the shoulder in a gesture of friendship.

"So you're not with this lot?" Taylor gestured towards the MPs.

"No, formally Naval Intelligence."

"Then we may just get along swell."

Taylor's teeth were gritted, and he had not let his guard down, but he already felt more comfortable.

"You are to be present for all contact I make with these two Krycenaeans, is that correct?"

"Yep, and they are members of $2^{nd}$ Inter-Allied and should be treated as such. Think of them as marines, and we'll all be just fine."

Weller looked into the cell and carefully studied the two of them. It was clear he had never seen one of the aliens alive before. Mitch could see he was a little unnerved by being so close to them and was unable to hide it.

"Have you really never had contact with a live one?"

"No, there's talk of a few prisoners around the world."

"Wounded? Were there really so few left behind?"

Weller nodded.

"They took everything they could with them. Most who were left fought to the bitter end. There have been plenty of reports of wounded creatures taking their own lives. Quite honestly, we have little information to go on."

"So this must a big deal? Why did you get chosen?"

Weller glanced over to Taylor and had a dismissive look.

"Yeah, right, classified information."

"Let's just say they wanted someone with combat experience, as well as the other tools of my trade."

Taylor lifted his eyebrows in surprise.

"Not just a desk jockey, then?"

"Come on, let's get this started. I'm more than happy for you to be in the room, but please do not interfere with my investigation."

The two of them stepped through into the room, and the soundproofed door sealed behind them. Taylor looked back to see as he expected. He couldn't see out beyond the walls of the cell. He knew the guards on the outside were watching in, but it pleased him to know that they couldn't hear what went on. Taylor's beach attire was incongruous in the sterile and serious cell, but both were glad to see him.

"I am Major Weller. I am here to try and answer the many questions we have about your... well, race."

They nodded in agreement. Both were sitting on the bench that ran the length of the wall. They were too tall to comfortably sit on the chairs nestled around the table in the centre of the room.

"Right, well we should get started."

"Don't worry about it," Taylor said. "Any information you can give could help, and once this is all over, you'll return to our unit."

"Worried? Why would we be?" asked Jafar.

Taylor crooked his head in surprise.

"Incarceration is never pleasant," he replied.

"There are many unpleasant things in life. Being locked in a room and asked questions is not one of them," replied the alien.

At every turn the Major got more an insight into how brutal an existence they had lived among their people.

"We have these things called human rights. Whilst you are not yet covered by such core principles, I hope you soon will be. They will protect you from any harm while you make no offence," Weller stated.

Taylor turned in surprise.

*A moral man, already looking to protect them. Not what I expected at all. I like this officer,* thought Taylor. He quickly realised that Weller could be a valuable asset to him in the future.

"Now, the first thing we'd all like to know is where you come from? Where is your homeworld?"

Taylor's ear pricked up at the word 'we', and he looked around to see tiny cameras in every corner of the room. It made him a little uncomfortable to know they could be watched by any number of people. He calmed his nerves and quickly thought he was foolish to think they would be alone. Their investigation would likely answer more questions about the enemy than they got answered during the entire war.

"Outside of our ruling classes, few of our people know much beyond the roles given to them, and explaining much of it in your language will be...challenging," Tsengal answered.

"Please try," replied Weller.

Jafar continued on from his associate.

"As protectors to Lord Demiran, we have seen and learned more than most. Do you have a star map?"

Weller tapped a few buttons, and the tabletop lit up. Within twenty seconds, the Major had a map before them. Jafar slowly stood up, and Weller looked up in amazement at the towering figure standing over him. Taylor could see a hint of fear at the realisation that the alien could crush and kill him in seconds. Mitch's trust of the two made him smile at Weller's discomfort.

The alien studied the map for a minute, carefully scanning and zooming throughout the display. He appeared to show little recognition or understanding at what he was looking at, but it was difficult to read some of his emotions. Sometimes the two of them appeared utterly deadpan. They waited with baited breath. It was one of life's great questions.

"All the years humanity has asked is their alien life out there, and if so, where? We might just be the first to hear the real answer to the latter," whispered Weller.

Taylor looked back to Jafar with a new sense of interest. The alien finally looked up.

"I have never seen your maps before, but comparing them to what I have seen, I would say our homeworld is here. In the system you call... Tau Ceti."

Weller turned to Mitch in surprise. His eyes were wide. It obviously meant something to him. To Taylor it might as well have been a made up name, for he had little care for anything offworld.

"We have long speculated that life could exist there. Although the living conditions must be unbelievably harsh."

He said it as he turned to the two aliens, looking at their

rock hard faces and strong stature.

"I think that much is true," replied Taylor.

"From memory, it is around twelve light years away. Even with the best technology we have seen yet, it would take them generations to reach us."

"Then maybe we haven't seen it all yet."

"That much is true. I just wonder if any of us truly want to see any more of them."

*Tau Ceti,* thought Taylor. *I'm sure that will not be the last time I hear that name.*

The questioning continued for several hours as Weller tried to delve into what knowledge they had of their homeworld and its surrounding colonies. It became quite clear to them both that the aliens knew surprisingly little about their own society. What little snippets of information had been gathered mostly as an aside to being the protection detail to an important Lord.

Taylor began to see how the two of them had so quickly taken a liking to him. He had treated them as he would a human being, something of which they seemed to have never seen in their previous lives.

Jafar and Tsengal painted a grim picture of their homeworld; a bleak rocky terrain with constant bombardments by meteor showers, and extreme conditions of which only the fittest would survive. Other worlds they knew of featured lethal gas atmospheres and temperatures that would kill you within minutes without the appropriate protection.

After this eye-opening discussion, Mitch could begin to understand why being held in that cell meant little to them. It was a life of luxury compared to all that they knew. Finally, as he felt his eyes sagging and his body sore, the other Major turned to him.

"I think this will do for today."

Taylor was surprised. He expected the interrogation to push for many more hours until all were exhausted.

*Why did they send such a decent man for the job?* He asked himself.

Mitch had never met any interrogator he liked one bit, but this man seemed different. He appeared far more human than he could have expected. Weller looked back to the two aliens.

"Thank you for your work today. Any and all information you can provide us will be vital in the future defence of us all."

"Then this can be our home?" asked Jafar.

"Most certainly. Any soldier who fights to defend our society deserves a place within it. You may rest easy for the rest of the day. I have arranged for you to have a few hours outside, but you must stay within two hundred metres of this complex. You will have a security detail with you at all times. I will return tomorrow."

He quickly stood up and nodded in appreciation to the two of them before making his way to the door. Taylor quickly followed after he had thanked his two friends. He stepped out of the cell to see Weller was waiting for him.

"I thought that went very well, and I look forward to working further with them."

"This is not what I had expected at all," replied Taylor.

"I know about your previous history, Major, and I can understand your feelings towards authority figures and the Military Police in general. What was done to you was very wrong, but do not assume for one minute that I am part of that crowd."

Taylor smiled, and they both turned and left the cells.

"Would you join me for a drink this evening?" asked Mitch.

"It would be a great honour."

* * *

A warm shower was a welcome end to the day's work. He stepped out and stood in front of the mirror. His wounds were all but gone from his body. He was still for a moment as he enjoyed the sensation of being both clean and unhurt. After a year in a state of pain and squalor, he had found a new appreciation for a peaceful life. He stepped out to his bedroom, reaching for his clothes when he realised someone else was in the room. Mitch's heart rate shot up. He knew a weapon was not to hand.

"A chance of a day of peace, and you're still working."

He turned to see Eli sat in the corner of the room. She looked far from amused, yet still glad to see him.

"Leave no man behind," he replied.

She shook her head in disapproval.

"How many times do we have to go through this? They are not humans, and they sure aren't marines. They are not your responsibility. Only a few months ago, they were probably killing our allies."

"After all they have done for us, they are my responsibility. We have been at war with many nations in the past, and yet we stood beside them in the last war. Anyway, I will have no more discussion about it. Jafar and Tsengal are members of our unit. We each rely on one another. If you cannot, I suggest you request a transfer."

Eli sighed in disgust and leapt up from the chair. She charged across the room and ripped the door open, leaving in a furious rage. He shook his head in response. Her overly dramatic response didn't impress him one bit.

"And to think I looked forward to this shit," he muttered.

He turned his mind back to the day's events and remembered he had agreed to meet Major Weller shortly. Mitch walked barefoot across the smooth floor, enjoying the relaxing sensation that was easing his mood. He tapped the button on his wardrobe, and the doors slid apart. Inside was a line of uniforms that were immaculately clean and had been untouched in a long time.

Mitch reached in for his dress uniform and realized quite how long it had been since he had last seen it, let alone worn it. A few minutes later, he was strutting across the base and looking a far cry from his bedraggled appearance from earlier in the day. Meeting Weller had given him a glimmer of hope for his future on the base. Despite being loved by so many of the serving marines, he was ever more hated by so many of his superiors and others in the service.

As he stepped into the mess, he could see Weller had identified him immediately and turned to the barman to order him a beer. He stepped up to the bar and thanked his new acquaintance.

"You sure know how to win friends," said Mitch.

"I didn't think I needed to."

Taylor threw back his beer and took a long relaxed sigh as he slumped down against the bar.

"Just when you thought it was all over, eh?" asked Weller.

"I never thought for a minute that this was over," he whispered. "We've humiliated an enemy which consider themselves infinitely superior to ourselves. Do you think for a minute that they would let it slide? They are down but not out."

"I have to say, you're not as I expected at all, Taylor. Your reputation made you appear as a glory seeker."

"Don't hold back now," he replied with a smirk.

Weller held out his arm in friendship.

"The name's Bryan."

Taylor accepted his gesture.

"Mitch, and for the record, you're not the pencil pushing stuck up bastard I would have expected, either. You are no stranger to this war, where were you?"

"New York, from the very beginning. I was liaising with the National Guard there when the invasion of the east coast began. I lost communication with my CO and jumped on the first truck I could find to take me to the front. We thought we could hold them there and then. We were wrong."

"You saw all of that, and yet you treat Jafar and Tsengal with such respect?"

"You do, don't you?"

"I have my reasons. You have none."

Weller raised his eyebrows and turned back to his drink, thinking about Taylor's observance. Bryan finally looked back to Mitch who was awaiting some answer.

"I guess it's my job to give these things a little more consideration. The automatic response of a human being now is to want to kill the aliens upon first sight, but isn't that what human beings have done to each other for thousands of years? We need to be a little more progressive. Somehow, you have managed to find allies among them. If two defected, maybe more could follow?"

Taylor shook his head. Bryan could tell that he was not

at all convinced.

"No? So what made those two so special?"

He remained silent for a moment. The moment they became his allies was still something he had not fully explained or shared with anyone, but he knew the time would come when he would have to do so.

"When we captured Lord Demiran on L2, those two lay down their weapons and surrendered to us. During the chaos of the attack on the station, they managed to escape, just as all soldiers have a duty to attempt."

Weller leaned in closer to hear Taylor's low voice.

"Go on."

"During their re-capture, an officer subordinate to me tried to execute them, despite not presenting any threat. Having saved their lives, that same officer attempted to take mine, and very nearly did. Those aliens saved my life. They did the right thing, but I can never go on the record with such information. We saved one another's lives, and in doing so have eternally earned each other's trust."

Weller took in a deep breath and sat up straight on his stool.

"Most interesting," he replied. "And you have told this to no one else?"

"Not the whole truth, no."

"And now those around you doubt your belief in our alien friends, and you cannot explain to them why you place your trust?"

Taylor nodded in agreement. He was impressed that the Major was so quick to understand the situation.

"You were right to remain silent. There would be a violent backlash if it became known that they had killed one of our officers, no matter how justified."

Taylor was still unsure of Weller's endgame, but he had a good feeling about the man. He surprised himself that he had come out so quickly with that story having never told anyone.

"You were quick to get that out of me, and I commend you. I only hope you use such information wisely."

"Those two could be vital in the coming years. We need all the help we can get if there is any chance of gaining more foreign support, or even creating dissent among their ranks. It could make all the difference."

Weller threw back the last of his beer and laid the bottle down on the bar.

"This is it for me. I have further notes to make, and we both need our rest. I will see you at 0900 hours at the cells."

Taylor nodded in agreement and lifted his bottle in a sign of friendship. As the Major walked away, Mitch thought hard about their newfound friendship. He'd never come to trust anyone so quickly before, and that still made him suspicious, despite not having any reason to doubt Weller.

He returned to his quarters to rest out for the night. The

room was silent, and it was clear Parker had not been back. As much as he'd have liked her there when he returned, he hated the fact she was being so unreasonable.

*It had been so much easier during the war,* he thought.

Climbing into bed alone was lonely, but it was just the tranquillity he needed to rest and recuperate. Mitch was finally feeling that his body was recovered from the brutal year it had endured.

\* \* \*

It was 0901 and the two officers were sat at the table, as they had been the day before. Only this time, Taylor's shorts and sandals were gone and replaced with more suitable attire. Weller read out his name, rank and others present for the records before beginning.

"Your former Lord Demiran and his kind. How did they get to their position of power?"

The two aliens looked confused, and Jafar finally spoke.

"What do you mean?"

"How did Demiran become a Lord?"

"He was born."

"Are all Krycenaeans status dictated by birth?"

"Yes, but you must still prove yourself in that class or risk being outcast."

"So you were both destined to be guards to a great Lord from birth?"

"They nodded."

"And what dictated that?"

"Our people come from one island on one planet. We are more intelligent than most, faster, stronger and more agile. We have guarded the Council of Lords for thousands of years."

Taylor sat in shock. He had never thought to ask any of what Weller was doing, but it was explaining a lot of what he had been curious to know.

"I would like to know more about your society, but we will come back to it. The Krycenaeans seemed desperate to conquer Earth at any cost. Under the command of Karadag, what was the purpose of the invasion?"

"The Great Book tells of a world so heavenly that any Krycenaean would die to live on it. Our people have searched for it for hundreds of years since our technology allowed us to do so."

"And you believe it to be Earth?"

"I believe so. It is the most amazing place we have ever seen. Clean sweeping oceans, free from radiation and meteor showers; temperatures that you can live in without fear of death, and no predators hunting you. This is a paradise."

Tsengal continued.

"Our Lords have gone from one system to another, destroying all in their path in an attempt to find such a place. Other races have fallen under the onslaught you faced."

The two men's faces went blank. It was so much information to take in; they could barely believe their ears. The room went silent for half a minute as they tried to picture what they were being told.

"My God," Taylor finally spoke. "They're systematically wiping out civilisations to find their perfect world."

Weller leaned in towards Mitch and whispered.

"We had suspected something of the sort for some time, but knowledge of other races is something we had no idea of."

He looked back to the Jafar.

"These other races you have encountered, have they been utterly destroyed?"

"That was before our existence."

"Damn shame."

Taylor butted in.

"The technology we have seen so far would suggest it could take hundreds or thousands of years for your ships to reach Earth, is that so?"

Weller initially turned to cut Mitch off, but he let the question stand, as he was inevitably about to reach the same one.

"For the first ships, the pioneers, yes. They left our worlds knowing that their future generations would reach their destinations. We now travel on the gateways they produced."

"Gateways? What do you mean?" asked Taylor.

"I think he means some kind of gateway through space, folding space, black holes..."

"You believe it possible?"

"Technically, yes."

"We cannot tell you how these work, only that a gateway was established a little over a year ago in your time, enabling the fleet we travelled with to reach Earth."

"This space gateway, it is still there now?"

"I do not see any reason why not."

"And you can travel through these instantly?"

"Yes, but they are built many thousands of kilometres from planets, for reasons we have never been told."

Taylor could not believe what he was hearing, but he knew it meant that the threat of a second invasion hung over them.

"How long would it take for a fleet to go from your homeworld to reach Earth?" he asked with urgency.

"A few days."

"My, God," he replied. "This changes everything."

Taylor stood up and looked to the nearest camera.

"You hear that? An enemy fleet could come through that gateway at any moment? We must destroy it!"

"Major Taylor!" Weller shouted. "You must calm yourself!"

"Calm? We were not prepared for the last war. Should we make the same mistake again, it could cost us our entire civilisation!"

"And nobody is going to let that happen. We will act upon this, and believe me, the appropriate powers will already be preparing a response, but we must not go into the next war blind."

Taylor took a deep breath and calmed himself as he sat down once more.

"This gateway threatens us all."

He looked to his two alien comrades.

"Tell us everything you know about it."

# CHAPTER THREE

"Form up!" Jones ordered.

Chandra rushed towards them at a brisk pace. They all knew that a battle was coming. She continued on down the line of the two companies until she reached Jones. He saluted as she approached. She stopped quickly and took a deep breath before balling out the news.

"As of 0700 hours I have been informed that an enemy presence remains in the solar system; a presence that could threaten our existence just as much as this time last year. This enemy will not, and cannot be allowed to remain!"

She stepped along the line as she took another deep breath and looked at the faces of the troops who could not believe that after all they had been through, more was being asked of them.

"The enemy we face is powerful, deadly and not to be underestimated. If they remain in our solar system, it is only for one reason, to carry out a second attempt to conquer Earth and our other colonies. I'll be damned if I'll let those alien bastards loom over us. We're going to Mars and beyond to finish them for good!"

Cheers rang out along the line. She knew she had stirred just enough energy among them to dig them out of the hole they all felt they were in. Many of those who stood there had been in the war from the opening week, and they all wondered how much more their luck would hold out.

"We're wheels up in one hour where we will meet the rest of the Battalion at L2. Grab your gear! We've got a war to fight!"

She nodded to Captain Jones. He jumped forward and barked his orders.

"Companies, you heard the Colonel. Fall out! Go, go, go!"

The formation of troops scattered to prepare themselves to leave their homeworld once more. Jones turned to Chandra and had to concede she was right. He never wanted to believe that the enemy remained in their solar system, but in the back of his mind, he had always feared it.

"You knew all along, didn't you?" he asked.

"Honestly, I had no proof. But I knew the enemy fleet had to have some access point into the system. If their ships could travel at light speed, we'd have known about it.

Whatever is out there, it is the answer to how they got to us, and it's an access point which must be closed."

"Do we have any more intel regarding what's up there?"

"Major Taylor knows more than I, and he'll fill us in when we reach L2, but I think it's all a little sketchy. With our experience, we will be leading this operation, but we'll have plenty of support."

"I'll believe it when I see it."

* * *

Taylor sat outside General White's office. He could hear vigorous discussion taking place within but could not make out the topic. He was finally ushered through. Two officers passed him as he entered. Their faces were red with fury, and Mitch could make out the fatigue in the General's eyes. He sighed as his head dropped into his hands. It was clear he hadn't noticed the Major entering the room.

"Morning, Sir."

White's head shot up, and he looked embarrassed for a moment before realising it was Mitch.

"Thank God. I've got officers crawling out of the woodwork insisting they must lead this operation."

"Enthusiasm is a good thing, is it not, Sir?"

"Up to a point, Mitch. You've made plenty of enemies, and all of them are most bitter that you're heading up this operation."

"But I am not in charge, Sir."

"No, but you might as well be in their eyes."

The General tapped a button on his desk, a section slid open, and a drinks tray with a decanter of whiskey and several glasses arose from the opening. Taylor didn't think lesser of White for taking a drink. He knew the stresses and work the General had fought through. He poured out a drink but didn't offer Taylor one. They both knew that as a field officer on duty, he could not accept it.

"At L2 you will rendezvous with Admiral Huber of the Liberty Battle Group. He will be in charge of the operation. Due to your experience, your Battalion will be there for the primary reason of commanding the marine forces aboard. Colonel Chandra will lead all infantry forces, with you as her second. Your Battalion will act as protection for the Admiral's carrier, the Washington."

"Protection detail, Sir?"

"The Washington is the Navy's newest and most powerful ship, the first of its kind. It was laid down just a year before the war began. It began production as a new super freighter, but was re-designed as a carrier as the war progressed. It has been given every upgrade possible from what we have learnt in this time. At present, it has a detachment of one hundred marines aboard, but that will not be enough should there come cause to defend it. This is a great honour you are being given."

Taylor breathed out heavily through his nose. He didn't like being left behind during operations to babysit the commander of the fleet, but he knew he had no choice. Before the war, the only Navy vessels were small frigates and escort craft, and yet now he was being ordered aboard the first space-based battle group in human history.

"Sir, I have just one request."

"Well, go on."

"Jafar and Tsengal, the two aliens under my command, they would be a great asset in this undertaking. We are investigating an alien presence and technology which we have never seen before, so they could be invaluable."

"As much as you might think of them as marines, they are not, Major."

"Then make them so, Sir. They have proven themselves as much as any under my command. Induct them into the Marine Corps, and let them continue to assist us in this war."

White sat back and took another sip of his whiskey as he stared into Taylor's eyes.

"Fine, but do not make me regret it. I will have them put on paper and assigned to your unit. There are many who will disagree with the decision, and you must mind your manners when they make it known."

"Affirmative, Sir."

"Yes," he replied sarcastically.

They both knew Taylor would never stand by and let an

insult go uncontested.

"Reiter will also be joining you as an expert adviser to Admiral Huber aboard the Washington. He has more understanding of the alien technology than any human alive."

Taylor nodded in acceptance.

"Will that be all, Sir?"

"Tread lightly, Major. We don't know what you'll face up there. We need to understand what we are dealing with. I wish you the best of luck."

Taylor saluted the General and left the room. He rushed out of the building and towards the cellblocks to find his two friends. As he approached the building, he caught sight of something bizarre out of the corner of his eye. A basketball match was in play with marines in exosuits. The hoops had been placed at six metres from the ground.

He stopped and watched as the players leapt great distances in a superhuman fashion. Then as one of them leapt up to one of the hoops and scored, he realised it was Jafar, and that Tsengal was not far behind. He quickly rushed to the game and noticed Weller and several MPs stood on the side watching.

"Quite remarkable, isn't it?" Weller said as he approached.

Taylor looked back at the match again as play continued, and he was left open mouthed for at least a minute.

"Incredible," he replied. Taylor snapped out of his

daze.

"I am departing Earth within the hour, and those two are coming with me."

"I'd need orders from General White to free them into your care."

A bleep rang out from his Mappad, and Weller lifted the device, looking surprised.

"You do have friends in high places, Major. Looks like they're free to go."

He lifted up a whistle and blew loudly, calling the match to a halt just after another hoop was scored.

"Jafar, Tsengal, you are hereby inducted in the Marine Corps. You are to report to Major Taylor immediately for operational duty!"

Jeers and cries of celebration rang out from the exoskeleton clad marines. Several patted the two aliens on the back in respect of their achievement. They stood silently, not knowing how to respond. Taylor watched in fascination as the marines passed them by and welcomed them as brothers. He didn't recognise any of them.

*If only Eli could have seen this,* he thought.

The two stepped up to Taylor and saluted in a perfect manner, having copied it from what they had seen others do. He reached forward and shook their hands to congratulate them. They grasped his hand delicately, yet could still feel an immense strength through their hands.

"We set off immediately. Follow me."

"Good luck, Major," Weller said.

"I'm sure we'll be seeing more of each other," replied Taylor.

Mitch turned and led his two newly enlisted marines to their landing zone where the two companies under his command had assembled. The Deveron awaited them with the newly promoted Captain Ryan on the ground to greet him.

"Always the first into the frying pan, ey, Sir?" he asked.

"I joined the Corps, remember!" he jested.

He looked around to see his marines loading all their gear aboard. He caught a glimpse of Eli. She noticed his stare and looked back. For a moment she smiled, until she saw the presence of the two aliens behind him. She turned and scuttled off. Taylor turned to his new friends.

"You're in the Marine Corps now. It's a great leap in becoming accepted in our community, and in our race as a whole, but there's a long way to go."

"You keep worrying about us fitting in. We only care about continuing to work for you."

"Is there nothing more to life than work?" he asked.

They looked to one another.

"I believe what you call comradeship. It is the only comfort we have ever known."

"Then you are in the right place. The Corps looks after its own. Load up, we head out shortly."

Eddie Rains stepped into view.

"All squared away?" asked Taylor.

"Bet your ass, Sir. I see you won through in the end," he replied, gesturing towards the two aliens."

"Yes, but their arrest was not without benefit. We've learnt a lot from the questions asked of them. In fact, this whole operation revolves around it."

"Then let's just hope they truly are on our side."

Eddie turned and strode aboard the craft. Taylor gritted his teeth. He trusted Jafar and Tsengal, but he knew the pressure was mounting on them all, to the degree that a tingle ran down his spine. He knew in the back of his mind there was still a chance they could be working for the enemy, but everything he had seen and heard told him there was good in them.

"Load up, we lift off in ten minutes."

They passed him and a few seconds later, Parker approached in a line with her kit on her back. Her eyes avoided contact. He grabbed her, pulled her from the line, and whispered in her ear.

"Whatever is between us, do not forget who is in charge."

"And do not forget who your friends are," she replied.

He sighed as he let her go, and she continued on to the ramp.

*What will it take to get rid of such bitter hatred?* He muttered to himself.

Within a few minutes, he was aboard the bridge, and

they lifted off. He never liked leaving Earth and still despised doing so. He turned to Ryan.

"The enemy, they believe this to be a paradise world. Maybe they're right."

The notion took Ryan back for a moment, but as a well-travelled Navy pilot, it quickly made sense.

"Of all the inhospitable places in space I have seen, I think they're onto something."

With the rapid speed of the Deveron, it was a matter of hours before they reached L2. As they approached, they could see the twenty ships of the Battlegroup orbiting the station. Ryan gasped as he saw the Washington. It was the first time any of them had seen the latest flagship of the US Navy. It looked just as it was, a hybrid of human and alien technologies.

"What a beauty," Taylor said.

Every ship of the Battlegroup dwarfed the Deveron. Every one of them was newly manufactured or extensively re-fitted.

"It used to take three years to construct some of those ships."

"War can be a rapid catalyst for change, Captain," replied Taylor.

"One day I will command a ship like that, but I do not begrudge Admiral Huber's task here."

As they approached the dock, a signal came into the bridge. The Admiral was projected before them all.

"Welcome to the fleet. You will all know that there is no time to waste. The fleet is ready to embark, are you clear and ready to join us?"

"This is Major Taylor. That is affirmative, Sir."

"Good, then have your captain dock with the Washington as we depart. Huber out."

The projection disappeared, and once again they could see out to the vast Battle Group.

"Dock? With that?" asked Taylor.

"I am informed the Washington carries three of this craft and has further docking facilities for two more."

Taylor shook his head in astonishment at the vast carrier. He could make out a dozen fighter bay doors on three levels of the port side that they were approaching.

"Then take us in, Captain."

The vast engines of the carrier roared to life, and it soared forward with the rest of the fleet surrounding it as they approached. Their pilot took them in on the landing procedure to dock with a bay that would half conceal the Deveron with the superstructure of the Washington.

Ten minutes later, the Major stepped out to be greeted by the XO, Captain Vega. He led Taylor to the bridge while other staff established the companies on board the vast carrier.

As he passed through the Washington, Taylor was astonished at quite how utilitarian it was. The armour plating was thick, and there were no windows in sight.

Much of the interior was bare metal and had yet to see a coat of paint or other finish. There was not a hint of luxury. The Washington was a ship built in haste to serve only one purpose – war.

"Not quite the luxuries of home, Major?" asked Captain Vega.

"Actually a reassuring sight. Our armies and navies had become soft over generations of peace."

The bridge lay deep within the bowels of the carrier, far from the gun batteries and aircraft hangars. From approaching the ship, he had expected to find a luxurious and lavish bridge, but what he discovered was as utilitarian as everything else he had seen. The XO introduced him as he entered. In the centre lay an operations table where the Admiral stood. The bridge was manned by just fifteen crewmembers and was a far cry from anything he'd been accustomed to in the Corps. Colonel Chandra and four other officers stood next to the Admiral.

"Welcome aboard, Major!" Huber said enthusiastically.

Taylor saluted and approached with a smile. It was good to see Chandra again, and he already liked Huber's approach to running his vessel. Mitch and the XO joined the others at the operations table.

"I am sorry to say there isn't much to tell at this stage. We have plotted a course to the destination that our experts have been given, based on the intelligence you gathered. It'll be a two-week journey at the very least, assuming we hit on it first time. A space gateway, I hear this thing called. A year ago, I would have called the whole thing nonsense, but we have all learned to be a little more open minded."

"Yes, Sir."

"I have already arranged to have your Battalion billeted here on the Washington. Make it your home."

"Thank you, Sir."

"It's an honour to have you aboard, but news of the two aliens among your ranks has already spread like wildfire throughout the ship. The fact you trust them goes a long way with me, but let's not be in any doubt, we still understand little about this alien race. They must prove themselves to me before I will place my trust in them. Many of the crew will be uneasy with their presence. It is a fact we will all have to weather."

"Understood, Sir."

"Good, square your kit away, and see to your marines. Tonight, after you dine, you will all join me for a drink in my quarters. That'll be all."

Chandra and Taylor stepped off the bridge together.

"You've been causing quite a stir," she said.

"Nothing new, then."

She smiled.

"And you get to continue the war you wanted," he added.

She stopped him in his tracks.

"I never wanted a war. I never wanted to continue

fighting. I only knew it wasn't over. I wasn't willing to lay down my weapons, knowing that there was more to come. I will rest easy when I know we have truly won and made our homes safe."

"And when will that be?"

"When the enemy can no longer present a danger."

Taylor shook his head. It was hard to believe now that it could ever be a possibility.

"This space gateway, or whatever it is. If we can destroy it, we may cut off their route to Earth for hundreds if not thousands of years."

Taylor nodded in agreement. It was an appealing idea.

"Let's not speculate just yet. I'd like to know exactly what we're dealing with before coming to any conclusions."

* * *

That evening the Marine and Army officers gathered at Huber's quarters for the drink he'd invited them for. The only other Navy officer was Captain Vega. He welcomed them in and sat down at a dining table, barely large enough for them all to fit. His quarters were spacious but hastily prepared. In the corner was his private office. It was decorated with naval weapons and particulars from hundreds of years gone by.

The dining table was of thick varnished hardwood; an antique and decadent feature, contrasting heavily against the rough welded and riveted structure and interior of the vessel.

"Good Evening to you all," greeted Huber. "I know several of you have not met."

He point around the table.

"Colonel Chandra and Major Taylor of 2nd Inter-Allied. Colonel Hicks of 2nd Marine Division, Major Klimenko of the 874th Naval Infantry Battalion, Major Warren of 42 Commando, and Colonel Chen of the 55th Infantry."

Taylor nodded in greeting to Chen, who he'd last seen during the battle for the Moon. Admiral Huber continued.

"As you all know, this is a fact finding mission, but with the possibility of an engagement of the enemy. This new ship is a boon to the fleet, but let us not be in any doubts, space combat is something that is in its infancy for the human race. This should be a predominately Naval operation, but we still have no idea of what we will find out there. No ship which has headed for Mars since the war began has made it back."

"What exactly are our orders, Sir?" asked Chandra.

"To investigate for any evidence of an enemy gateway into our solar system. We are to seize control of any assets if the opportunity presents itself."

"Sir, if this gateway does exist, it threatens the safety of Earth for every moment it is allowed to remain."

"That is a consideration, Colonel. The possibility of destroying the enemy's access point into this system is one that was discussed, during a remote emergency summit held with world leaders just last night. I am in favour of doing such, but many within the Navy feel we should not destroy a major asset."

"Major asset? It might as well be a doomsday weapon if it allows the might of the enemy forces to be on our doorstep in a matter of days," replied Taylor.

Huber nodded in agreement.

"As much as that might well be true, we cannot make any decisions without the facts before us. It is also not our decision to make. It is a joint operation of Earth forces, so our elected leaders must decide on this."

"Surely this is a military matter, Sir," Chandra added.

"Ordinarily, yes, but there is no precedent for such an event. They will have competent military advisers to hand and can make their decision based on the information we provide."

"And if the enemy engages us?" asked Hicks.

"We can defend ourselves without recourse," replied Huber.

Taylor shook his head in disbelief.

"I wasn't aware we had to adhere to the rules of engagement against this enemy."

Huber took a calm sip of his drink and sat back as he eyed up the Major, evaluating everything he saw.

"It is not for the enemy which we follow our rules of engagement. We are going after a device that is completely unknown. We must know what we are dealing with before we make any brash moves."

Taylor rested back in his chair and knew that the Admiral was right. He could not bear the thought of another alien invasion, but also knew that haste could be the end of them all. Huber continued on.

"Colonel Chandra, your Battalion has been assigned this carrier. You will work in close correspondence with me, and I believe Major Taylor and your two alien marines could be a great resource to us. You will remain in an advisory position, as well as fleet defence, should we be at risk of boarding action. Keep your people sharp, and be ready for anything. We've probably got an uneventful couple of weeks ahead of us, but we are going into the unknown, so keep your guard up."

As the evening came to a close, Taylor finally made his way to the individual quarters that had been assigned to him. As he turned a bend in the corridor, looking for the number of his door, he stopped at the sight of Eli sat against the wall and clearly waiting for him. She looked tired and must have been there for more than an hour.

"I don't want to fight with you anymore," she whispered.

He nodded in appreciation.

"You've put your trust in me before, so do it now. I trust Jafar and Tsengal with my life, as much as I trust you with it. You must do the same. Inter-Allied is more a family than we ever knew in the Corps."

She did not disagree. He could see she had come to the realisation that she must put her past scruples behind her. He strode up to her and slumped down on the floor of the hard metal corridor.

"So did you learn anything interesting?" she asked.

"Not really. Only that Admiral Huber seems a good man and a good leader."

She looked at him in surprise.

"I know. I don't hate all of our Generals, just the idiots and bastards."

He got to his feet and hauled her up to him. He passed his ID card through the lock of his quarters and entered to find it was barely bigger than a closet, but at least he had a bed. They collapsed together and enjoyed the new peace they had found.

Ten days passed quickly with regular drills and exercises carried out on the Washington. Taylor had got into such a routine that it almost made him forget they were in space and hunting down alien positions. He had spent many years on board seaborne carriers and smaller vessels.

On the eleventh day, Inter-Allied was digging into their breakfast when red beacons began to flash and sirens rang out. Everyone froze, looking around for some explanation. A voice came over the intercom. It was Huber.

"This is the Admiral speaking. We have just received confirmed reports from the Kittyhawk that enemy positions have been identified. We are presently changing course and making an approach with caution. All personnel are to go to combat stations. All advisory staff should report to the bridge."

The room erupted into action with Navy, Marine and Army personnel quickly responding to the order. Taylor rushed to Chandra's side as she strode quickly for the armoury where their gear was stored.

"Huber seemed pretty insistent that we should join him now."

"And we will," she replied, "but not until we are appropriately equipped for any eventuality. We were placed here not just as advisers but also as protection for this carrier. We cannot provide that protection unless we are ready for action at a moment's notice."

"No arguments here."

As the two of them pulled on their exoskeleton suits, they watched Jones and the other company leaders organise the troops.

"Strange, isn't it?" said Taylor.

"What?"

"Not going with them. We are field officers. Our job is out there at the front."

"I'd be careful what you wish for, Major. We could yet have to get our hands dirty in this affair."

Fifteen minutes later, they reported for duty on the bridge. Huber initially looked up at them in an agitated fashion because they had taken so long. He calmed down when he realised he now had the protection they needed. He beckoned for them to come forward while looking in astonishment at the two towering aliens following them. The security detail initially stopped their entry and looked to the Admiral for clarification.

"Let them through!" he yelled.

The Navy guardsmen looked up in awe as Jafar and Tsengal strode past.

"You must all appreciate how unorthodox this is; armed soldiers from different nations, and aliens among them on the bridge of the capitol ship of the fleet. We live in a new age where such things change."

Taylor nodded in agreement and appreciation that they stood with such a forward thinking leader. He drew their attention to the display on the operations table. Chandra gasped at the sight of what she could see. Taylor stepped up to her side, and his eyes widened too.

Despite the enemy ships between them, it appeared to be what they were searching for, and they could make out the shape of the gate. It was a vast octagonal structure floating in space. Blue lights pulsed around the rim, and the framework expanded back as if presenting an entrance. Yet the gate was hollow at its core, and they could see nothing but space beyond.

"Christ. How big is that thing?"

"Five kilometres wide," replied Huber.

"Fuck me," whispered Taylor.

"Then Tartaros cannot have come through here," Chandra said.

"I would not jump to any conclusions just yet, Colonel. We all saw the expansion of that vessel when it reached Earth. There is no reason why it could not have been brought through in a series of parts."

"It would make sense," Taylor agreed.

Huber looked up at the two aliens stood on guard behind Taylor.

"You two. Step forward and tell us what you know about this."

Without hesitation, they both took several paces forward to the edge of the table.

"This is the gateway we came through."

"Are there more like it?"

"A few, but not in this solar system."

"That's a relief," replied Taylor.

They were all quiet for a moment as they stared at the vast and terrifying structure they approached.

"Something of this magnitude must have required years to build, and God knows how to reach this place."

"Our ancestors set off with these gateways hundreds, and some thousands of years ago from our homeworlds. We only know they have reached their destination of the gate in Tau Ceti, which they are connected to and is activated."

"Fascinating," he replied.

"And your race did all this to find the perfect world?" asked Chandra.

Tsengal shrugged his shoulders.

"We did it because we were told we must and that it was our duty. I can tell you no more," replied Jafar.

Lights flashed on the live display below them that caught all of their attention. They looked down to see engines firing up on multiple ships between them and the gateway.

"Looks like they've spotted us," said Huber.

"What do you want to do?" asked Chandra.

"Nobody touches the gateway."

He tapped a display on the table beside him, opening a channel to the fleet.

"This is Admiral Huber. Commence attack vector Alpha. Do not, I repeat do not, fire upon the gateway. If you discover gun batteries enclosed with the gateway, you are to withdraw out of range and continue to engage enemy craft. Proceed with caution, and good luck to you all."

He ended the transmission and turned to Jafar.

"Anything you can add here?"

He looked over the map.

"I know little about these gateways, but I can tell you that each of those ships will have two hundred soldiers aboard, with detachments of either fifty or a hundred in each of those smaller vessels."

"Bloody hell, there must be more than two-dozen of the larger craft," stated Chandra.

"But no capitol ships, so they have comparatively little firepower."

"What will their tactics be?" asked Huber.

"The ships are mostly intended for deploying infantry. They will not run. They will try and board us."

Huber turned quickly to the pilot. "How far out are we?"

"Twenty kilometres, Sir."

He quickly looked back to the map.

"Our guns are accurate up to almost ten, and they are based on enemy technology which is similar from what we have seen. Bring us to a halt. If they want to close the distance, we will not do half the work for them!"

"Aye, aye, Sir."

He opened up a channel to the fleet once again.

"The fleet is to hold position. Launch fighters, fire when in range."

"If they jam our signals, which they are sure to, what is the procedure?" asked Chandra.

"Fleet officers have already been briefed on the protocol for such an event. We stand and fight. No one is to withdraw unless we lose forty percent of the fleet, or are in immediate danger of doing so."

*A grim outlook, but its also a sensible contingency.* Taylor thought.

"Weapons are charged and ready, Sir. Fighters are launching in thirty seconds."

"Fighters in space? Not something we've ever seen," whispered Chandra.

"No, but the requirement became apparent. They are a heavy fighter design, and with three crew that borrow heavily from alien technology, as all this does," mused Huber. He pointed to everything they were wearing.

Huber looked away from the table and back to his crew who all looked to him.

"Display tech projection."

The walls around them blurred and then sprung to life. The entire CIC appeared to evaporate and displayed everything outside the ship as if they were now floating in space. Taylor felt sick for a moment, and almost instinctively reached for his suit helmet for the environmental control and air.

"Amazing, isn't it? We've had this tech thirty years and never really needed."

Chandra paced around the room, inspecting the fleet. It felt as if she could simply reach out and touch the other ships in their fleet. Then she turned and looked towards the pulsating of the engines of the approaching craft.

"For the sake of simplicity, we will call the larger enemy ships frigates, the smaller ones destroyers," stated Huber.

Fighters burst out from the centre of the room and into view. They were joined by smaller detachments from the surrounding vessels. The enemy were just minutes away, but it felt longer as they soared towards the human fleet. Taylor leaned in over Chandra's shoulder.

"I wasn't made for this, to sit in safety at the back," he whispered.

"When any of those ships get through our defensive fire, and they will, you can bet your arse that marines will be all that stands between victory and defeat."

Taylor smiled. Huber turned to them both and nodded in agreement. He paced closer and whispered to them both.

"If the Washington is breached, we only have enough marines to cover so much ground. Chandra, you are in charge of any internal defence of this carrier. Look after her, she's fresh out of dock."

"We'll hold, Sir."

"Sir, the enemy will be in range within thirty seconds."

"Prepare to fire!" Huber shouted the order.

Just seconds before the first enemy craft entered range, a huge pulse of light burst from one of the enemy ships. A beam of light stretched out from the vessel and instantly struck the Maryland, one of the frigates in front of the Washington. The ship was torn in half with debris pouring from the hulk. They could see the silhouettes of dozens of bodies thrown out into space.

Huber froze in shock at the sight for just a few seconds then turned to his gunnery commander.

"Fire now, everything!"

Lights flashed from them, lighting up space for kilometres around the carrier. Pulses flashed back and forth as the enemy continued to rush towards them. Three of the enemy frigates and two destroyers were obliterated in the initial burst, but it didn't slow the rest down.

Huber turned to the two aliens in the room.

"What the hell was that weapon?"

"Nothing we have ever seen," replied Jafar in a concerned tone.

It was the first time Taylor had ever seen the alien show concern.

"You didn't think we were the only ones developing our technology, did you?" asked Chandra. "We've given them a hard time. They're not going to take it lying down!"

Another beam tore through one of the human ships, but to their horror it came from a different enemy vessel. Huber looked closely and could see the vast barrel protruding from the enemy ship, and there were two others like it. He tapped his console and barked out his commands.

"All Battlecruisers target those gunships!"

"Sir, we've lost all signal to the fleet and have internal solid feeds only!"

"God damn it! Concentrate all our fire on those things!"

A volley of fire smashed two of the enemy craft, but they watched in horror as the third got a last shot off before it burst into flames. The pulse hit the hull of the Washington and caused the lighting to dampen and flicker. They were thrown violently about the ship and the tac projection vanished, leaving them with the bare metal walls of the bridge.

Taylor lifted Huber back to his feet. Blood trickled from his face. They looked around for the others just as the emergency lighting system came online.

"Status report!" called Huber.

There was no response for a moment as the bridge staff tried to make sense of it all.

"Sir, we've taken heavy damage across floors thirteen through eighteen. Breaches have been sealed, but we still have fires on multiple levels."

"Casualties?"

"We don't have that much information yet, Sir."

"Get me some eyes on the battle!"

The operations table he rested on lit up and flickered, finally coming to life. Taylor clambered over to the table in time to watch in astonishment as two enemy craft smashed into the Washington.

"Jesus Christ!"

"Sir, we have multiple breaches on floor three and eight!"

Huber turned to Chandra.

"We'll keep the guns firing. Do not let this ship fall!"

"What about the bridge, Sir?"

"We have enough guards to look after us. Get to those breaches!"

# CHAPTER FOUR

Lights flickered as power fluctuated throughout the Washington. Engineering and medical crews rushed about their duties. Taylor and Chandra fought through the chaos with Jones' Company in tow. They now wore their full helmets with independent oxygen supply, so they could be ready for anything. The Colonel stopped at a junction and looked down two of the corridors feeding onto it.

"God damn, it all looks the same," she whispered.

"This one," replied Taylor.

"You sure?"

"No, but we have to keep moving."

"Alright, go!"

They rushed forward down yet another corridor they'd never seen before. Taylor held is Mappad forward and tried to make some sense of their location. It shook about in his hand. He reached over, clipped it to his left forearm, and continued. It looked like they were heading the right way, but in the desperate rush and in a maze of corridors, it was difficult to know.

"I think we're about a hundred metres away!"

As he said it, an explosion ripped through the corridor only ten metres from their position. The massive impact threw them off their feet, and the hull of a smaller enemy vessel smashed through into their corridor and passed right through into the next. Even before Taylor could get to his feet, he was sucked through a hole in the breach and out into space. He looked back to see the corridor had been shut off and its atmosphere normalised. He could see Chandra stood looking in horror as he floated away. The blast skin closed up around the hull of the enemy vessel, instantly sealing the breach.

"Fuck sake!" he shouted.

He'd never been tossed out into space before, and it was an oddly frightful, as well as fascinating, experience. He knew his suit and its integrity were all that was keeping him alive. But he turned and could see the whole battle before him. Several of their fleet had been hit by boarding actions, but the fight continued to rage. Enemy and friendly fighters soared about between the larger vessels, and pulses of light zipped across the sky. It was a fascinating light display, like watching fireworks.

Realising he needed to get back to the fight, he hit his boosters which instantly brought him to a halt and put him back on course for the Washington. He stared up and down for some way in. The nearest airlock was fifty metres from where he had exited. Within a minute, he was up to speed and descending towards the door at speed. He landed and saw they were thick blast doors that he'd never get open. There was no lock and entry system in sight, but he could see a small camera monitoring the door. Taylor manoeuvred his head in front of the camera.

"This is Major Taylor. Open the doors!"

He got no response.

"Open the fucking doors!"

Still no response, and fear began to set in. He knew his air supply would not last forever. He turned back to the enemy ship and thought about his options. He could see it was already damaged from various pulses on its way in.

"Alright you bastards, I'm coming for you."

He leapt off from the Washington and hit his boosters once again. As he soared towards the ruined hulk, he fired in rapid succession at one of the damaged parts within its hull. He got off just ten shots and hoped for the best. He tucked his legs under and forwards so that he was going feet first. Mitch hit the structure hard, but he burst through and tumbled into the interior of the enemy vessel.

There was no obvious sign of life. He staggered to his feet and looked around. The interior had the same utilitarian and sterile feel that he had become accustomed to seeing. Then something caught his attention - a display screen with two routes from their current position and to the CIC.

"My, God. They're going for the bridge!"

Footsteps broke the silence, and he quickly lifted his rifle so see a Mech in light armour step into view. Its weapon was slung low, as if seeing a human was the last thing it expected. Taylor did not hesitate to take advantage of his position and fired four shots into its chest. The armour penetrating Reitech rounds punched right through its thin armour and out the back of the creature's body. It tumbled to the ground, and Taylor made a quick sweep of the room and its two exits. The dead alien had little equipment or heavy weaponry. He quickly came to the conclusion that it must have been the pilot.

Then he remembered the map he had seen and rushed over to take another quick glance.

"Christ," he blasphemed once again.

Mitch leapt into action and rushed out of one of the exits, heading in the rough direction of where he thought the breach into the Washington could be found. He finally found it and rushed out into the carrier, to be met by two shocked soldiers of Ota's Company. They lifted their rifles rapidly when they saw his figure tumble out of the enemy vessel.

"Sir, what the fuck is going on?"

"They're going for the CIC. Where is the Colonel?"

"Some way down this corridor, we believe."

"Alright, find Ota or Jackson and tell them to get as many of your Company back to the CIC immediately. You must protect Huber and the bridge!"

"What are you gonna do, Sir?"

"Try and hunt the bastards down from the other side. The Mechs that came from this ship are going for the heart of the Washington. Now go!"

They turned and ran, as did Taylor in the opposite direction. He could hear gunfire intensifying up ahead and knew he must be in the right place. A few minutes later, he reached a junction where Chandra and Jones were huddled, trying to defend from a stream of Mechs. Jafar and Tsengal were fighting at their side.

"Colonel!" he shouted.

She fired a few more shots before realising who it was. She turned in surprise and relief that he was alive.

"How on Earth did you get back?"

"Doesn't matter. The Mechs are going for the CIC."

"What? How do you know?"

"That doesn't matter either. If they can take control of the bridge, we'll lose the command of this fleet, and they'll turn the guns on the rest. Control of the guns of this ship could end us all!"

"Fuck! Do you know where they are now?"

"I've got an idea, yeah."

She spun around. "Jones, I need a platoon, and you two."

She point to the aliens. Taylor was surprised she was so keen to have them at her side, but they all knew what an asset they could be. The Captain shouted for the nearest unit to follow the Colonel.

"Lead the way!" she yelled to Taylor.

They passed down two corridors and could hear fighting throughout multiple sectors, but they could spare little time to assist anyone.

"You really believe they are going for control of the ship?" Chandra asked.

"Outnumbered and facing superior firepower, wouldn't you? They aren't fighting to the death, they are fighting to protect the gateway!"

They came to an abrupt halt as half a dozen Mechs turned a bend up ahead and continued, not having noticed them. Taylor quickly took advantage of the situation and lifted his rifle, pouring fire into their backs. The broad corridor allowed six more of the platoon to join in. The creatures were riddled with bullets but still managed to turn and fire a few pulses. One rushed over Chandra's head, the other skimmed the hip of one of the privates, causing him to squirm in pain as he collapsed to the ground.

Another volley of fire finished the creatures for good as Chandra knelt down to the wounded man. She took a quick look at his wound and grasped his shoulders, peering into his eyes.

"You'll be fine! We cannot stay here or be slowed down.

You keep your rifle at the ready, you hear?"

The Private was still stunned, but he nodded in agreement. Chandra hated leaving one of their own behind, but she knew there were bigger things at stake.

"Let's move!"

She leapt forward and led the platoon right over the bodies of the Mechs. Wisps of smoke still rose from their thick armour where the Reitech rounds had drilled right through. As they passed along more corridors, they found the bodies of several of the ship's crew and no sign of life.

*Shit, we need to get a move on.* Chandra thought to herself.

She upped the pace and within a few minutes, they could hear gunfire once again. It was a welcome sound, as it meant someone had stood their ground against the incoming enemy.

"How do you want to do this?" Taylor asked.

"No subtleties, we just keep going forward."

They passed several corridors that they recognised and realised just how close they were to the bridge now. Taylor was thankful it had been placed at the core of the vessel. He was certain the carrier would have fallen to the enemy if it had not been. They took a turn up ahead and were met face-to-face with several creatures at the back of their column. Chandra and Taylor fired a quick few bursts and ducked back as pulses smashed into the wall where they had just stood.

"Guess we found them!"

"Best thing we can do from here is to keep up the heat," replied Taylor. "The more trouble we cause, and the more of those bastards we can take down, the better chance we give Huber."

Chandra dropped to one knee and edged around the corner, and Taylor stood over her. They fired two bursts each and quickly ducked back. They hoped they'd taken one of the creatures down but didn't have enough time to confirm it. Just as they were about to repeat the process, they heard panicked shouts echo from the back of their platoon, followed by gunshots.

"Incoming!" they heard down the line.

"Stay here and keep firing!" shouted Chandra.

She jumped to her feet and rushed down the corridor to find four of the platoon firing down a side corridor from either side of its entrance. One of the women leapt back to reload, and Chandra ducked in beside her.

"How many?"

"I saw a dozen, but there must have been many more with them."

"They're going for the CIC, and we're blocking their path," she replied.

"Yes, Ma'am."

"We cannot retreat, and we're fighting both ends. Whatever happens, do not let them pass!"

The Private nodded in horror. The Mechs were still advancing relentlessly, no matter how many they cut down.

The Colonel got to her feet and retreated to her previous position where she found Jafar joining in the action.

"Something's got to give," stated Taylor.

"When you were out there, Mitch, how many breaches did you see?"

"Three for definite, maybe four."

"Then we must have now encountered three of those assaults. We must hope Grey got to the other."

"This was a grave underestimation of the enemy strength. Somebody made a big God damn mistake," Taylor shouted.

"You got that right, but we're giving harder than we're getting. As long as we can stop the bastards getting into the CIC, we will still pull through on top."

She pulled a grenade off her armour and placed her hand over the arming cap.

"You think we should be using those here?" asked Taylor.

"It's far from ideal, but the alternative is far worse. I'll take the chance."

She twisted the cap and launched it rigorously down the corridor, ducking quickly back around next to Taylor.

"Fire in the hole!" she yelled.

They hunkered down and counted the two remaining seconds before an ear splitting explosion rang out down the corridor. The walls at their backs shuddered violently. If it weren't for their enclosed suits, they'd already be deaf.

For a moment, Chandra sat motionless in shock at how the enclosed corridor had intensified the grenades impact. She didn't want to look around and see what damage she might have caused to the fleet's prize vessel. Taylor laughed at her shocked face.

"Right on, Colonel!"

He stepped past her and peered down the corridor to see four Mechs lying dead from the blast. Several others were badly wounded or incapacitated. Chandra leaned in to see the result and breathed out a sigh of relief.

"Pass the word. Use the grenades."

Taylor rushed off down the line and continued to relay her orders until he reached the other end of the platoon, where the troops were still firing frequent bursts in an attempt to stop the Mechs. He peered around to see that they had gained another ten metres on them. He pulled out a grenade, primed it, and tossed it down the corridor.

"Christ!" one of the soldiers shouted out, and they ducked back.

The explosion sent vibrations through the walls again, and Taylor just prayed that any collateral damage was worth the result. The enemy corridor went silent for a moment, but it was then filled by another grenade exploding further down and punctuated by a hail of Reitech rifle fire. Taylor looked back down the troops alongside him.

"Hold your fire, lads. That's friendlies coming in."

He peered around the corner to see the last of the

creatures cut down by dozens of rounds. Several rushed past and hit the wall close to the Major. A few moments later, he could make out the silhouettes of Exoskeleton clad troops jogging down the passage towards him. Lieutenant Grey was at the forefront.

"That's some damn good timing, Lieutenant!"

"Thank you, Sir. We've dealt with one of the other assaults already, but we believe there is still at least one in the wind."

Taylor pointed down the corridor.

"At the other end of here, trying to fight their way to the CIC."

"Shall we..."

"Damn right."

Taylor stepped confidently down the corridor to the Colonel with Grey's Company close behind. She turned and marvelled at the reinforcements and the realisation of where they had come from.

"Alright, lads. Let's cut these bastards down!"

She lifted her rifle and stepped out in the corridor in plain view of the enemy. The broad corridor allowed many more of the troops to flood in and open fire in a brutal onslaught. They walked towards the enemy, cutting down all before them. In just thirty seconds, they had killed twenty of the beasts and were still advancing forward as most of them changed their magazines. A bend up ahead concealed the rest of the enemy force who were engaged in a brutal battle with the defenders at the entrance to the bridge.

"We need to watch the crossfire," Taylor whispered.

"I know, got any grenades left?" replied Chandra.

"Just one."

He looked across to the others and could see three others still had some high explosive.

"Anyone with grenades. Be ready to use them!" Chandra ordered.

Taylor turned and walked backwards, so he could address them.

"Friendlies on the other side, beware of their fire and of your own!"

As they reached the corner, one Mech turned the bend, trying to either fix or reload his cannon. Chandra fired six shots into its chest without hesitation, and Jafar let off a single bullet into its head.

"Grenades!" Chandra roared.

Taylor led the way, pulled out his grenade, waiting with his other hand on the firing cap. Four others joined him.

"On three. Three, two, one."

They twisted the caps and launched them all around the corner. Chandra knew it was a risky strategy, even more than the first few they had used. The massive explosion rumbled the corridors, sending shards of metal into the air that embedded in the corridor wall in front of them. The heat was enough to feel even through their suits.

Taylor immediately drew out his Assegai and leapt around to finish off any that were left alive. Just five creatures remained standing, two of which appeared stunned or hurt. He rushed the first one. It was disorientated, and he drove his weapon into its stomach and high up through its body. Out of the corner of his eye, he caught a glimpse of Chandra leaping forward in a similar manner.

One of the creatures swung its weapon around, but it was too slow and clumsy. Taylor ducked under with a nimble roll and drove the Assegai into the armour at its thigh. The Mech tumbled over, almost crushing him. He ripped the weapon from the beast's leg and blood gushed out across the deck. He reversed the Assegai and drove it down into its faceplate.

He stood up and turned to see that the enemy were done for, and all attention had turned to his personal combat. The thick dark blue blood he had become so familiar with poured down his gloves and armour, though he could not feel it.

"All clear?" called Chandra.

The silence was broken by footsteps and the troops parted. Taylor stood up and took Chandra's side as he saw Huber step through to greet them. He wore a pistol on his side but was as steadfast as ever. He stopped for a moment and looked around at the carnage the battle had created. Several of his staff rushed in with extinguishers to put out the small fires the grenades had ignited. Huber shook his head at the wreck the flagship had become.

"Sir, all known enemy assault craft have been accounted for, but there could yet be more," stated Chandra.

"Thank you, Colonel. The battle is over. We have destroyed or disabled all enemy craft. Our comms are still being repaired, but we know the Endurance, Chicago and Helena are gone. Many others have received severe damage. The Washington is still under her own power, but we will need weeks of repairs before we can get back into service."

"It's a bitter price for victory," whispered Taylor.

Huber just about heard the Major and looked up to see he was genuinely sorrowful for the losses of many he had never met.

"Indeed, Major, but we came here for a fight. We will mourn our losses, but we must now look to the future. I want you and Colonel Chandra to join us on the bridge, and keep a dozen marines with you. Have the rest of your Battalion run sweeps of the vessel. I want to know for certain we are not carrying anymore unwanted guests."

"Not all here are marines, Sir," replied Chandra.

"You are now," replied Taylor with a smile.

She turned to Lieutenant Grey.

"I want you to take the upper ten decks. Send runners to find Jones, Ota and Jackson that they are sweep the remaining sectors, thoroughly."

"Yes, Ma'am."

The former Staff Sergeant shouted out his commands as if he were trying to deafen the Colonel before turning and barking further orders to his Company. They rushed on to carry out their new duties.

"We need to get communications back online ASAP, Sir."

"Agreed, Colonel, we're already doing all that we can. The jamming they ran is a God damn nightmare."

"Yes, Sir," Taylor replied with the voice of experience.

Huber nodded and sighed at the same time.

"I know you are no stranger to this, Taylor. All the experts we have back home have been working round the clock on a way to block their jamming signal, but quite frankly, we still aren't sure how it works."

Within seconds of him speaking, the ship's comms officer turned around and broke the news they were back in contact with the fleet. Huber leapt into action.

"Alright, send word to Command that we have located and secured the area surrounding the space gateway. We have sustained damage and losses in doing so and will maintain positions to allow time to repair and refit."

The three hundred and sixty degree display of their surroundings fired back up to life, and he stood open mouthed as he experienced the results of their battle. Two of the ships they had lost were now floating hulks. The other two had been blown into multiple parts and were now nothing more than debris. Half of the remaining ships in the fleet showed major battle damage.

"There must be survivors out there. Send out any shuttles and transports we have and get the rest of the fleet to do the same."

"But, Sir, we can't spare the personnel. We're having trouble enough handling the repairs," replied Vega.

"I don't give a damn. There are personnel out there who may have precious little time left."

Huber turned back to their operations table where Chandra and Taylor awaited him. Taylor already liked the fleet's leader, but he prayed Huber would be able to maintain his control over the fleet in the face of such devastation. He tapped a few buttons on the table display, and it turned to the gateway.

"Just look at it, a marvel of technology, and yet used for such evil."

"It must be destroyed," replied Taylor.

"I wouldn't be so hasty to burn all our bridges. That gate could be humanity's great leap out into the universe, which it has so desperately pursued."

"You surely can't want to go through it?" asked Taylor in shock.

"You're damn right I do. Sure we could destroy it and forget this all happened, but if they could build the gate once, they'll do it again."

"But that could buy us decades or even centuries of time."

"Living in fear that they will one day come back, no thanks. We've started a job, so let's finish it."

Taylor could understand her position, but he knew what it would mean – the deaths of hundreds of thousands or even millions in a more bloody war than the last.

"Right now we can't do anything," replied Huber. "But I want to know we have that gateway secure. Clearly it has landing bays, and it must be crewed. I want you, Colonel, to organise an assault to capture the gateway. You have two hours to complete your sweeps of the Washington, and then you will carry out these orders."

"Sir, the gate could open up anytime, and God knows what's on the other side. We should destroy it now when we still have a chance," pleaded Taylor.

"We all have our orders, Major. There is to be no attempt made to sabotage the gateway unless such orders are received to do so."

The room went silent for a moment before Taylor finally remembered his brief moments aboard the enemy craft during the battle. He leaned in close so that only Huber and Chandra could hear.

"During the boarding action, I got a glimpse aboard one of the enemy vessels, and it is likely still there now, embedded in the hull of the Washington. They had a precise and accurate layout of this vessel and a well-planned path directly to the bridge here. I fully believe they intended to gain control of this ship and turn its guns on the rest of the fleet."

"What? How could they have such information?" asked Chandra.

Huber shook his head in astonishment.

"The plans of the Washington were carefully guarded from the moment the conversion began," said Huber.

"We have no idea how their technology work," replied Chandra. "Maybe they have some kind of surveying equipment which mapped out the ship as we arrived."

"Maybe, or maybe someone is providing the enemy with information," replied Taylor.

"What?" Huber asked. "Why? Who would do such a thing?"

"It's a serious allegation," mused Chandra.

"I don't know why and wouldn't like to imagine we had people working with the enemy, but it's happened in all other wars."

"Right now, we have no proof or even leads to go on. This isn't over, but let's look to the task at hand. Good luck to you."

\* \* \*

Taylor and Chandra sat opposite each other aboard Rains' Eagle HV as they cautiously approached the space gateway with another eight such craft.

"You really think this thing can fold space?" Eddie

asked.

Neither of them answered him for a moment. They stared at each other, trying to make sense of the other's perspective. Both were curious about the gateway, but they had vastly differing perspectives on what they believed should be done with it. It was the first time they had ever come to a disagreement about the way forward, but there was no ill feeling.

"Guys? What's the deal?" continued Rains.

"You know as much as us, Eddie!" Taylor answered.

"I doubt that," he muttered in response.

Chandra looked sympathetically towards Taylor. She could completely understand his desire to end it all there and then, but she also knew they had a responsibility to the future of humanity.

"I don't want to go on fighting, you know," she said quietly.

Taylor barely heard what she said, but the few words he caught and the look on her face tallied up.

"I know. Who knows what the right answer is here? When we look back on this in years to come with hindsight, then we'll know," he replied.

"Those bastards came close to bringing humanity to extinction. If we let off now and let them come back stronger, do you really believe we could survive? Maybe we'd never see another war in our lifetime, but in another fifty, hundred or two hundred years, that would be the end.

Could you go home and back to your old life, knowing we have forsaken the next generations?"

Taylor shook his head. He no longer knew what was the right course of action, but at least he was among friends. He simply smiled in response, and he thought deeper about their conundrum.

*We're still speculating without all the facts,* he thought.

"How come they ain't shooting at us?" asked Rains.

Taylor and Chandra leaned forward to look out of his cockpit. In the depths of their conversation, they had forgotten they were approaching the enemy gateway. Lights still faded in and out around the device, but there was no sign of any opposition to their landing.

"Landing in two!"

They watched as he took them in to what was clearly some sort of a landing bay. It was easily large enough for all of their craft to dock, but only five of Eagles swooped in on the initial wave. None of them could believe they had not yet been fired upon. They passed through the vast cavernous entrance and were beginning to get an understanding of just how vast the structure was.

From a distance, the landing bay looked tiny, but now they could see it was the scale of the gateway that had made it appear so small. The gateway was the size of a substantial moon. As they put down, they noticed the landing bay was completely empty.

"Looks like there's nobody home," said Taylor.

"I don't like it," replied Chandra.

She turned to Jafar who was sat just a few seats away.

"Where is everyone? Could this vast structure be unmanned?"

"Could be. I have never seen inside one of the gateways, but certainly it is a possibility."

The craft touched down, and Chandra was quickly out of the door before anyone else. She peered around at the aliens' docking bay. It appeared uncannily similar to one of their own bays. Most of the structure was made of slab sided metal, and it could only be described as spartan in design and layout.

"I don't like this at all," whispered Taylor.

"It's more than a little creepy. Do you think it's possible this thing runs itself?" she asked.

"Why not? We have more and more unmanned machines and facilities on Earth. This is probably just a bay for maintenance crews."

"I'd like to know for certain that we are alone."

Taylor looked around, remembering quite how much the structure dwarfed them. He peered around for any ways out of the docking facility.

"It could take weeks or even months to search this thing."

She sighed as she realised he was right.

"Alright, we'll have to maintain a presence here, though."

"Agreed."

Taylor shook his head as he panned around the area.

"What is it?" she asked.

"Just that I was expecting a fight."

"Sorry to disappoint you."

She turned to Captain Jackson.

"I want you to continue to investigate what you can, and keep a constant watch here. Make sure to keep an eye on your oxygen tanks, and refill them from the 'copters at regular intervals. You'll be relieved in six hours."

"Yes, Ma'am!"

Taylor and the Colonel climbed back aboard with Rains and slumped back into their seats. It should have been a relief to them not having to fire a shot, but none of their questions had been answered.

"Back to the Washington, Lieutenant!" Chandra ordered.

"Damn quick visit!" he replied.

"Fleeting certainly."

"We could have stayed and investigated further," mused Taylor.

"That's not our job. We came here to secure the landing area and deal with any hostile forces. We will maintain guard for now, but it's time for the appropriate experts to take over. What the hell do we know about such things?"

"A damn sight more than most," he retorted.

Chandra thought about it for a moment and then looked

around the docking area again. She shook her head.

"No, experts like Reiter and his people were brought on this mission for a reason. We need to leave it in their hands to make some sense of this... thing."

There was a brief silence as Taylor tried to understand whether she was marvelling at the technology or disdainful of it.

"To use it or destroy it?" he asked.

"That's not a decision we can make anymore. We can send in our recommendations, but ultimately, we are here to follow orders."

"And that's okay with you?"

"Okay? When have we ever had to like our orders? We will do whatever is decided for us. Now, this appears to be in hand. We can leave it to Jackson. World leaders will want our reports on this without any further delay."

It was not long before they both sat in Huber's quarters. The first transmission would still not reach earth for several days, leaving them in an anxious position.

"Acceptable losses and the enemy gateway in our hands. This was as successful as the mission could have hoped to be," Huber said, but he sounded tired.

*Acceptable losses?* Taylor thought. He hated the term, but he could see that so did the Admiral.

"What now, Sir?" asked Chandra.

In a few days, Earth will learn of our success here, but we cannot wait for the endless back and forth messages which we must endure this far out. I am sending representatives back to report in person, and that will be you two."

The two of them were stunned. They were both combat officers. The immediate understanding of the pressure that would be placed on them set in.

"Surely there are other officers rather more suited to this liaison task?" she asked.

"With a better way with words, yes, but you were there in the thick of it. You both have more experience facing this enemy and their technology than anyone in the fleet. We're quite literally in uncharted waters here. I want the reports to be made by those it affects most. As frontline veterans, you will be asked to fight should we step through that gate. I cannot think of a more honest pair to analyse this situation."

They accepted his assessment and argued no further.

"We will maintain position here until further orders. In the meantime, we have a lot of repairs to undertake and that will give our scientists and engineers time to give this gateway a good look over. I will hang on to your Battalion for the defence of the Washington, if I may. They have proven invaluable."

"Of course, Sir," she replied.

"Take the Deveron and two platoons for protection, and get back to Earth with all haste. We will continue to transmit all news and information to the Deveron as we get it while you travel. Lay this story out straight. There is still a lot to learn here, but we already have some major decisions to make."

"Understood, Sir."

"That'll be all. Get underway as soon as possible, Colonel."

They stood up and silently left the Admiral's quarters, pondering the new responsibility they had been given. They reached the end of the corridor at the elevator when Taylor finally spoke.

"We're both being sent to make this report, but we do not agree on the correct way forward."

"Do you not think that is a good thing? We are being asked to report and advise, and in that duty we have a responsibility to give both sides of the coin. Do not change your opinion just because I am in command of the Battalion. I believe I am right, but I am sure you think just the same of your own strategy. We can't honestly know who is right at this stage. Let's not fight over it."

Taylor nodded in appreciation of her understanding. Chandra tapped her comms unit and was glad to find it working once more.

"Captain Jones, be at the Deveron with two platoons in the next ten minutes. Have them fully geared and ready to travel."

After a few seconds of silence, Charlie came on the line with a surprised tone to his voice. "Uhh…yes, Ma'am."

"We travelled all this way and now going we're going all

the way back," whispered Taylor.

"I have no doubt we will be back shortly."

Taylor hoped not. He was fully intending to recommend destroying the gateway and the enemy's access point to the solar system. He imagined he was going back to Earth for good, but the possibility of other paths was quite frightening.

"You know we fought and won on our own soil, who is to say what lies beyond that gateway?" he asked.

She nodded in agreement.

"Have Jafar join us. Have Tsengal join Captain Jackson aboard the gateway. They might be able to help at both ends."

They arrived in the docking bay where the Deveron still lay to find Captain Ryan with his feet up, playing a game of cards with his bridge crew in the vast docking area. They had stacked up some crates to make a table and used others for seats. Ryan looked genuinely surprised to see them approaching.

"Every time I see the two of you, it always means we're heading for trouble," he jested.

"Not this time. We're heading home to report on everything we have seen, and you're our chauffeur," Chandra answered.

Jones briskly rushed into the room with his troops in tow. He held his rifle at the ready as if he expected a fight. Chandra was glad to see he was naturally as cautious and ready as ever. He relaxed as he approached and saw their casual conversation.

"We're heading back to Earth, Charlie. I am leaving you in charge of our forces on the Washington. Captain Jackson will be your second and preside over any duties aboard the gateway."

Jones looked confused by the news.

"The fleet is staying here. We're reporting back, and we'll see where this goes. Have your men get aboard the Deveron and prepare for departure. We will return in a month's time, perhaps more."

She could see he had many more questions, but he didn't waste time asking them. He turned and sent the troops forward into the Deveron before making his goodbyes. She didn't like leaving almost everyone she knew at the enemy gateway, knowing that at anytime a fleet may come through it.

"Good luck," he said.

She turned to Ryan.

Have your crew square away. We're heading for Earth."

# CHAPTER FIVE

The Journey home was even more tedious and mind numbing than the route they had taken to find the gateway. Chandra and Taylor were sat on the bridge, both knowing they would soon see their home. Up ahead, the Moon shone brightly like a beacon calling them back. As they drew nearer, a transmission came in.

"Deveron, this is Commander Kelly."

A video display flickered to life. The battle-hardened officer displayed a smile as he could clearly see Taylor and Chandra on the screen.

"Good to see you again, Sir," replied Chandra.

"Likewise," followed Taylor.

The Commander was displayed on a small projection beside the larger view of the Moon before them. As they drew nearer at a rapid speed, they could see a mass of ships orbiting the Colony.

"You see them, don't you?"

"Sir?" asked Chandra curiously.

"The next battle group, and almost ready to join you."

They could make out fifty ships already. The massive dockyard of the Colony was packed with hulls and partially completed ships. They could see many of the craft were freighters that had previously been used to transport goods and people between Earth and the Moon. Others were exploring vessels. All had been undergoing a refit to prepare themselves for military service. The vast fleet dwarfed what they had led out to the gateway only a month before.

"My God, how did you do it?" asked Taylor.

"Not alone," he replied. "The powers of Earth have combined to work hand-in-hand around the clock. These are wartime conditions. You would be amazed at what can be achieved when things are desperate."

"Ain't that the truth?" Taylor added.

"We have all heard the news of your defeat of the enemy fleet. Congratulations on your victory."

"Thank you, Sir, but it was not without loss."

"It never is, Colonel. I have been called to an emergency meeting on Earth, along with our Prime Minister. I assume that has something to do with your arrival?"

"I believe so," replied Chandra.

"Then I'll see you both shortly. Good seeing you again."

The transmission cut out, and Taylor remember just

how thankful he was to have made an ally of Kelly.

A few hours later, they were making their descent to Camp Pendleton where they could see dozens of civilian transports lined up in the main landing zone, awaiting their arrival. There was no victory parade organised for their landing, only an officer and few guards to escort them to inside the main conference hall.

"Not much of a warm welcome," said Taylor.

"What were you expecting, the President to be there to give you a medal? We won an important victory at the gateway, but it is only the first step."

Upon landing, they were greeting with an abrupt 'follow us'. The soldiers parted Taylor and Chandra from the others who were clearly not allowed to follow them inside.

"I have been lumped in with these kind of talks before," Taylor said quietly. "They are long, tedious and rarely take any heed of advice from people like us."

"Maybe you just didn't tell them the right things."

Taylor grinned and laughed just a little.

They were led into the conference hall where world and military leaders from all major powers had assembled. It was an intimidating sight for the two of them. Taylor always hated the formality used in politics and the higher-ranking officials. They were announced and then asked for an immediate report of the events they had taken part in. For two hours, the crowd listened intently with Chandra doing almost all of the talking. General White finally stood up as they drew to a close.

"Thank you, Colonel, and you Major. You may take a seat."

The General strolled up to their position at the front to address the crowd. He had become one of the key faces in the war against the alien invaders and had naturally risen to the task of administering the conference.

"Shortly before your arrival here, we received a transmission from the Washington that the scientist Doctor Reiter believes it unsafe to attempt to dismantle or destroy the space gateway. He believes that such tampering could have cataclysmic effects for our solar system. Essentially, we do not know enough about the technology to attempt such a feat. He does, however, believe its operation is very simple."

Taylor turned in shock, but it was clear that the rest of the audience had already been informed of this information.

"I believed from the very start, as did many of my staff, that all attempts should be made to destroy any route into our solar system. That option having been taken off the table, we are now at a fork in the road. If we cannot stop them coming here, we must either take a defensive strategy, and prepare for a future attack, or take the fight to the enemy. My opinion, ladies and gentlemen, is that we should not stand back and hope for the best. I believe we should step through into their world and stick it to 'em whilst they're on the run."

"Thank you, General."

The President of the United States, Adrian Walters, stood up and took the floor.

"We have all suffered a great deal in this war. The world has suffered to the degree that it will never be the same again. But, it has brought a unity that this planet, this solar system, has never known. The United States' position is that we cannot, and will not, stand by and go about our normal lives when an apocalyptical threat hangs over us. We will take the fight to the enemy!"

Cheers of support rang out around the room. But President Moreau stood up in opposition. The hall slowly fell quiet enough that he could be heard.

"My country of France was ravished in the last war, worse than most. We cannot ask more of our people. We cannot support such warmongering, nor are we willing to lose more people in another pointless war."

"Fucking idiot," Taylor murmured.

General White heard him but was glad no one else did. He did, however, share Taylor's belief. He shot up from his chair to address the Frenchman.

"I was not aware, Mr President, that any human faction could be considered warmongers. I also seem to remember that when your country was threatened many nations, whose leaders stand before you today, went to your aid.

You are here today because the world supported you. Will you not give anything back to protect all our futures?"

The French President's face went red with anger and rage.

"Millions of French citizens and soldiers died in the last war! What more can you ask of us? We have won! Let us return to peace and our normal lives, and forget the troubles which are now over!"

Taylor shook his head as Chandra leaned in to his side.

"Naive bastard, how can he turn a blind eye?" she whispered.

They watched in amazement as several world leaders cheered in support for the Frenchman.

"It's easier to pretend the problem doesn't exist rather than deal with it," he replied.

"Then you are in favour of going through the gate?"

"If it cannot be destroyed, yes, it is our only option."

She smiled to herself. *Taylor is back on side.*

The American President stood up once again, and General White called the room to silence. Walters was a tall but thin and wiry man and in his early seventies. His hair was a shiny white, but he still had a full head of it. He was a staunch republican, and a man who had clearly lived a hard but successful life; his face heavily wrinkled and rough. He stood tall and proud; a man who was strong in the head even if his body no longer was. His suit was of a cut not seen in fifty years. This man was as a relic of a bygone era.

"You have all heard the facts. The United States is committed to the safety of this planet and that of the Lunar Colony. And to that end, we will do whatever is necessary to protect them. In four weeks, we will send a fleet through the space gateway, with the intention of taking the fight to the enemy. We need all the support we can get. I ask you all to dig deep into your conscience and appreciate how vital this mission is to us all. Now I ask you, a show of hands. Who will join us in this enterprise?"

The British Prime Minister and German President were first to raise their hands and voice their support. A number followed until the final divide was set. A third of the leaders in attendance remained silent, still including Moreau.

"Then it is decided," stated White. "We have a majority support for action. I thank you all for your support in this undertaking and would ask you to have your Generals liaise with myself immediately. I hereby call this conference to an end!"

Taylor could see the disappointment in Walters' face. They had enough support, but he had clearly hoped to rally world leaders as one. Those who had not voiced their support quickly stood and left the room. Most of the others broke out into conversation with the people around them.

"This divide will not end here," said Chandra. "Many

have shown their true colours. If they falter at such a time, then we would do well to keep a keen eye on them."

"What do you mean?"

"I mean, Mitch, that we should not assume that all mankind is on our side. I do not say they would ally with the enemy, but they would certainly act in hindrance of us."

Taylor nodded in agreement. He had seen such during the war. After they had given everything, it amazed and disgusted him that politicians walked away as if they had the moral high ground.

"Ignorant bastard!"

He said it loud enough that several around them heard, but he didn't care. General White paced up to the two of them with a sigh.

"It is done then."

"Nothing is done, Sir. This is the beginning of a long road," replied Taylor.

"Has any progress been made on improving Earth's orbital defences?" asked Chandra.

White nodded hesitantly.

"Yes, but I am not sure anything we can do would withstand the overwhelming power of their first assault. That is the nature of static defence. The best thing we can do is to develop our fleets. With another few months of all-out construction, as we are doing, I believe we could have enough Navy power to fight them out there and away from our colonies."

"Then the Marines' role will be more important than ever. This enemy pursues ruthless and fearless boarding actions that are devastating. Maybe just a hundred or two got aboard the Washington, and we came close to losing her, and perhaps the rest of the fleet."

White looked at them in shock.

"Taylor is right. It was no plain sailing."

"And yet you still support the decision to go through the gate?"

"I don't see that we have an option anymore," replied Taylor.

It was clear to them both the General was genuinely surprised to hear that they were not convinced by their chances of success, yet they wanted to go anyway.

"We've got three weeks. Soldiers are not a problem, veterans and recruits alike. Since the war ended, a continuous recruitment campaign has boosted the Marine Corps to numbers none of us have ever known. But what we now need so urgently is ships. The dockyards of the world are working around the clock, but ultimately, those on the Moon and L2 and L3 are the key players."

Neither of them answered as they awaited more convincing words from the General.

"I know we are sending you into the unknown, but not without every ounce of support than can be given. I have already volunteered to join the Washington as leader of the Marine forces within the fleet, a request I have do doubt will be accepted."

Chandra turned and peered into the man's face in surprise. It was clear he had every intention of doing so.

"Then I suggest you get some combat training in, Sir. You'll almost certainly need it."

White nodded in surprise.

"Major, yes, yes, of course. Now, Colonel, there is work to be done. This new fleet will embark in three weeks. I want you both to return to the Washington. I have already gathered together personnel of Inter-Allied who have recovered and are ready to re-join your ranks, as well as a few dozen experienced marines to redress your numbers. They'll be at the Deveron within the hour."

'Thank you, Sir."

They left the building with their escort to find Jafar and the two platoons they had brought. They were still waiting for them beside the ship. It wasn't long before the promised reinforcements turned up.

"Fucking great," muttered Taylor so that only Chandra could hear.

She looked up to see that Suarez was among those approaching. They both knew he was trouble. Neither wanted to promote him or even accept him as a platoon leader, but he had been with them from the very start.

He led the thirty plus marines who approached as if he owned them and was coming to the rescue. He had a broad sleazy smile across his face.

"Good to be back!" he shouted, making a rather casual salute on approaching.

Chandra didn't make contact with him, choosing to address the incoming troops as a whole.

"No time for niceties. Load up, we are moving out!"

Taylor smiled at the Colonel's dismissal of Suarez's arrogant greeting which shot him down in flames.

Within fifteen minutes, the Deveron was lifting off once more. Chandra and Taylor both attended the bridge, partly to see Earth one last time as they departed and partly to escape Suarez. They knew he was going to be a problem they would have to deal with, but neither could face it there and then.

\* \* \*

Five weeks passed before they finally got word of the fleet's approach to the gateway. There had been little training to do for the troops of Inter-Allied. They passed the time with guard duties and familiarisation of the ship they were stationed aboard. Chandra and Taylor were called to the bridge for the announcement of the arrival of the mass of new vessels. A cheer rang out across the ship as Huber announced it over the comms.

"Just look at it," called Huber. "The grandest fleet ever amassed."

They looked out to space with the Washington's projected display. They could see more than fifty sizeable ships, including a carrier not so different to the Washington.

"How on Earth did they manage it?" asked Huber.

"I hear that construction on some of these began just weeks after the war on Earth ended. They weren't built in three weeks," replied Chandra.

"No, but impressive nonetheless, Colonel. Before the war, it would have taken the dockyards three years to build such a fleet, and they'd have been unarmed. All this is in less than a year."

"Amazing what the human race can achieve when it's against the wall," Taylor commented.

"Sir, we have a shuttle coming aboard."

Huber turned to the two Inter-Allied officers.

"Please join me."

They arrived at the docking bay in time to see the ramp lowering on a brand spanking new shuttle. General White stepped aboard with several other Navy officers they didn't recognise.

"Welcome aboard, Sir!"

"Thank you, Admiral Huber, let me introduce you to Admiral Uxbridge of His Majesties Royal Navy, Commander of the fine new carrier you see out there, the Trafalgar."

"My compliments."

"Tell me, Admiral, is expert opinion unchanged

regarding this space gateway?"

"Reiter and his team of experts still believe they can operate the device, but are a long way from understanding how it works or how, or if, it can safely be dismantled."

"Then the only way is forward. It's been a long journey out here, and I suspect your crews are as anxious for a change of pace as well. Are we confident about the stability and operation of this device?"

"We have already carried out tests with drones and safely been able to send them through the gate and recover them. The fleet is ready for immediate departure."

"Excellent. Admiral Huber, you will remain as Commander of this fleet. Admiral Uxbridge being second. I will maintain command of infantry forces from here on board the Washington. I now pass over command to all forces to yourself and wish you every luck on this new undertaking."

"Thank you, General."

Huber lifted his comms unit and tapped it.

"Prepare the fleet for departure. Begin a thirty minute countdown and have Reiter synchronise."

The command staff returned to the bridge with General White. It was an anxious waiting game as lights flickered and flashed around the gateway. Taylor and Chandra had missed the previous tests of the gateway, but they could see the bridge crew were still as mesmerised by it as they had been the first time. Taylor leant in over General

White's shoulder.

"Assuming this leads us into enemy territory, what then?" he asked.

"We strike at the enemy in any way we can. Hit the first targets hard and keep moving forward."

"And what then? Do we try and take them to extinction, like they did us?"

Chandra could hear the conversation and leaned in to give her two pennies.

"Probably a damn good idea."

White shrugged his shoulders.

"We need to remove the threat they pose. If we can do that by winning a few victories and showing them we are all powerful, great. If not, we keep pushing, and we do so until they can no longer endanger our lands. If in the meantime, if we can find a way to dismantle that gateway, we'll take that option."

The gateway suddenly pulsed with a violent burst of light and spun into life. The entire gateway began to rotate at a slow and steady pace. Beams of light darted across the core of the huge ring until they filled it in a giant swirling ball of blue light. It was beautiful and almost magical, but they could not help feel fear for what might be on the other side.

"One giant leap for humanity and all that," whispered White.

The light faded to the centre until it was almost white,

and the structure began to spin faster as the swirling core increased in velocity.

"The gateway is ready for entry, Sir!"

Huber hesitated for a moment. It was a frightening step into the unknown. He took a deep breath and breathed out slowly. He gave the order.

"Take us through."

The engines of the Washington fired up, and they slowly ambled towards the swirling wall of light. Three frigates of the fleet were ahead of them, and they watched as the bows of the vessels pierced the light and continued on through as if vanishing into fog. Many on the bridge held their breath and felt fear overcome them, but they knew they had passed beyond the point of no return. The Washington pushed on through. Taylor's right hand slipped over the grip of his rifle that rested on his flank. He didn't like passing through into the unknown without being prepared for anything.

Eventually, they were through the swirling light. For a few moments, they were bombarded with strobes of bright white light that the ship's display quickly dimmed to accommodate. In just ten seconds, they rushed out into the black of space once more. Many sighed in relief and looked around to see the fleet coming out behind them.

"That wasn't so bad," Chandra said.

Huber spoke up.

"Scan the area. I want a full status update on our

location."

The only light in the area was provided by the gate itself and the lights of the ships of the fleet. Like the other end of the gateway, it had been built far from any sign of life.

The comms officer spoke, but there was shock and disbelief in his voice.

"Sir, we are in the Tau Ceti system. The computer is still gathering data, but our maps are mostly accurate for this system already."

"How far are we from the nearest inhabitable planet?" asked Huber.

"All planets in this system are hostile to life, but they may yet support it. I believe we could reach the first in twenty-eight hours, Sir."

"Then plot a course, and open a channel to the fleet."

"Yes, Sir."

The room was silent as they awaited the Admiral's announcement."

"This is Admiral Huber speaking. We have now entered the system we refer to as Tau Ceti, named after its sun. We are almost twelve light years from home, and a distance the human race could barely comprehend just a year or two ago. Now we have travelled that distance, which is no small thing. Under any other circumstances, this would be a feat worth celebrating, but we didn't come here to explore, or to mine, or to colonise. We came here to fight, and I fully intend on doing so."

He took a deep breath before continuing. Several of the bridge crew nodded and murmured quietly in support.

"Admiral Uxbridge and half of the fleet will remain here to guard the entrance to gateway. Orders and status updates are being updated as I speak. Remember, that if the enemy cannot get through this gate, they cannot reach our homes. The Washington will lead the rest of the fleet to the nearest planet that we believe to be an enemy colony. Today we bridged the gap between our civilisations. Tomorrow, we make them pay for what they did to humanity, Washington out."

Taylor still stared out into the depths of space. Up ahead, they could see the glimmer of stars and planets. The nearest appearing as a similar size as the Moon viewed from Earth. He had expected to step into a whole new and different world when they passed through the gateway. It was an anti-climax he was actually glad to have experienced. Huber turned around to address them.

"We're heading for that planet to cause merry hell. There may also be much to learn on the enemy's own soil. You can bet that we'll need troops on the ground. Have your people ready."

"Always, Sir," replied Chandra.

The days and weeks of travelling were making them all feel utterly exhausted. Space travel had been limited before to the extent that few ever passed beyond the Earth's Moon and the LaGrange stations. Taylor sighed as he yawned.

"We should both get some sleep," Chandra said. "We aren't needed here for a good few hours, and we'll certainly need our strength when we arrive at our destination."

Taylor agreed with her. He wasn't going to fight about it. They strolled off the bridge together.

"I know you didn't want to tread this path, Mitch. But you should know I would never have chosen it if I thought there was a better way."

"I appreciate that. It just seems that whatever happens, we are always thrown in the shit. Isn't it about time we were laid up to rest, and others took on the work?"

"We aren't the only unit on this mission. The fleet is packed with soldiers and marines."

"Mmm," Taylor muttered, thinking about the most recent troops to join them. They had both been ducking Suarez since he had returned. "You know this Grey-Suarez situation needs to be resolved?"

Chandra sighed at the very thought of it.

"Follow me. Let's get this over and done with."

She carried on to the elevator, lifting her Mappad to check the unit schedules. She quickly learnt that Grey and his Company were carrying out hull breach drills. She hit the button in the elevator and stood silently. They rapidly descended to the Lieutenant's level. When the doors opened, she stormed out at a quick pace with Taylor in tow. As they took a bend, they could see Grey up ahead.

He stopped his unit and called them to attention.

"Lieutenant Grey! In recognition of your fine services during the assault on the space gateway, for your continued fine service, and under several recommendations, I am hereby giving you a field promotion to Captain. Your papers will be put in order on our return home, and your pips will be delivered to your quarters with the hour."

The British former Staff Sergeant was flabbergasted.

"Well, what have you to say for yourself?" prompted Taylor.

"Thank you, Ma'am."

"Carry on, Captain."

She turned and strode quickly back to the elevator, leaving Grey still motionless and shocked by his abrupt promotion. When the doors of the elevator closed, Taylor finally spoke up.

"That wasn't exactly...by the book."

"What in this war is?" she replied.

"Oh, I hear you. It's a band-aid fix to the Suarez issue. The fact you promoted one of your NCOs over him will probably just piss him off further."

"Probably, but I'd rather have him pissed off than hounding me. I can promote whom I bloody well choose, and I just as rather Suarez had stayed at home. How you ever tolerated him, I will never know."

"You can't choose every officer in your command."

"More's the pity. I am sick of dealing with morons,

cowards and idiots."

Taylor was taken aback by her sudden outburst, but he didn't want to pursue it any further. He had gotten himself into enough trouble in the past as it was.

"How about getting that rest?" he asked.

He could see the weary look in her eyes. They both knew a battle was coming, and neither of them wanted to go into it already fatigued. Taylor barely remembered much from this point on. He stumbled into his quarters and had just enough time to strip off his exoskeleton suit before dropping into bed with his uniform still on.

Fourteen hours later, he awakened and looked in shock at his watch. It was more sleep than he'd gotten in years, and it was an odd sensation to arise naturally. But within just a few minutes of sitting up, a warning alert blared out from the speaker in the corner of the room. A voice was calling him to the bridge.

*"This is finally it."*

The Major hauled on his equipment and rushed to Admiral Huber's side. He entered the bridge to find Chandra already there, and she didn't have the recently awoken look he sported.

"Did we wake you, Major?" she asked with a smile.

He looked out to the display screen to see a zoomed in picture of the planet they approached. It was a reddish-orange and appeared dry and rocky. The surface looked jagged and bombarded with space debris, but amongst it all, he could make out the uniformed structures of buildings created by intelligent beings.

"Have your alien friends join us. They may be of help," ordered Huber.

They all stood and marvelled at the display, trying to imagine how it would look and feel to stand on an alien world. They didn't have the technology to scan for much in the way of useful information at such a distance, but they could still peer at it through their ship's telescopes.

Jafar and Tsengal stepped in, and it was clear they had been standing guard outside. They stood and stared for a moment, the same as the rest present.

"What can you tell us about this planet?" asked Huber.

"It is Krycenaean, but not a world we have ever seen."

Huber turned in surprise. The prospect of not recognising a planet inhabited by your people was truly an unknown concept to the humans, but he could see in their faces, they did not lie. He stayed silent and let them continue to investigate what they could see. Finally Tsengal spoke.

"Neither of us have ever travelled to this world, but it certainly is not an important colony."

"Not important in terms of life or resources, or what?" asked Chandra.

"I could not say. Only that we have never encountered it."

Taylor looked to Chandra with the same curious

expression Huber displayed. They all wondered if the planet was of little importance to the alien race, or of great importance and kept a secret.

"Whatever it is, we're heading right for it. If we are going make any progress in this star system, we need to gain some ground."

"I'm just not sure what is worth fighting for down there," replied Taylor, looking at the barren landscape.

Huge caverns divided rocky outcrops on a dry scarred surface. As much as they were all curious to set foot on it, the planet looked far from hospitable.

"Would a planet such as that have any kind of defences? What about troops?" asked Huber.

Jafar shrugged his shoulders.

"Never having been there, I do not know."

"Then I guess we're going in blind."

They caught glimpses of movement from the planet and watched as entrances opened on the surface. Small craft poured out towards them.

"I guess we have our answer. Launch fighters! Alert Admiral Uxbridge that we have made contact with the enemy!"

He turned back to Chandra.

"Have your unit ready to go. I don't think we'll have too much trouble with this lot, and I don't want any delay in reaching the surface. Be ready to embark at a moment's notice."

Taylor's eyebrows raised at the dismissive nature of the forces opposing them, and he only hoped Huber's confidence was founded in fact. Chandra grabbed his arm and led him from the bridge.

"Stay near a comms unit in case we have need of you!" Huber shouted as they left.

The two of them rushed to the armouries. Jafar and Tsengal were close behind.

"Make sure to load re-supply crates aboard all ships and copters. I'll be damned if we're going to an alien planet without enough ammunition," Chandra shouted.

"Still think it's such a good idea? I mean we won on our own soil, but fighting over the enemy's own territory is a completely different story."

"Yes, it is a different story. We'll give them a taste of the pain and suffering they brought to our world. These creatures are not as all powerful as they believe themselves to be. Their technological advances are quickly being matched, and they cannot withstand the adaptability and will to survive of the human race."

They arrived at the Deveron's docking area to find Jones had already assembled the Battalion. It half filled the vast facility. Ryan and his crew were formed up behind them and wearing much of the same equipment.

"Thank you, Captain. At ease!"

She strolled quickly to the centre of the formed up troops.

"Up ahead is an enemy planet. We don't know what it's called, and we don't know what is there. It appears to be a small colony on the fringe of the star system we know as Tau Ceti. It may or may not have strategic value. We are all going into this blind. What I can say for sure is that it's high time we pushed them back, and it's time they were made to suffer. Inter-Allied are to be feared by all our enemies. This is our time!"

Cheers rang out, but they quickly went silent as all were unsettled by the uncertainty they faced. The Colonel paced along the line, and she could feel her pulse increase. It was the only thing that would calm her. Just a few minutes later, they heard the ship's guns open fire.

"Listen to it. That is the sound of payback. Remember when we first faced them two years ago. Remember how scared you were when they rolled into our lands, all guns blazing. That is how they'll be feeling today, and when they run, we'll chase them!"

Taylor didn't much care for Chandra's bloodlust, but he could understand how it was useful to settle the troops and get them in the right mindset. He looked to Chandra, and she smiled back in response. So close to combat, their own squabbles seemed to melt away, and they both wished they had not wasted such time on them. Eli would never be happy with aliens within their ranks, but she knew she had no say in it. An enemy pulse crashed into the Washington on a floor above them, causing a breach. Blast doors shut down near the entrance to the docking facility as emergency beacons flashed.

"We must be close now!" Chandra shouted out.

She hoped Huber's confidence was founded, and that they were still on track, but the honest truth was she wasn't convinced. Taylor leaned in over her shoulder as she paced past him.

"Think we can make it to that planet?" he asked.

She shrugged her shoulders.

"I bloody well hope so."

They listened for fifteen minutes and stood patiently as the combat raged around them. They could all tell the engines were still roaring and driving them forward to the enemy planet. They took it to be a good sign, but none were sure.

*Damn waiting game,* Taylor thought.

Finally, a light repeater flashed on a wired comms line on the wall beside where the Colonel stood. She hit the accept button.

"Colonel Chandra?" It was Huber.

"Yes, Sir."

"We've all but cleared 'em out. Load up and begin a countdown. You lift off in five minutes."

"Affirmative, Sir."

She turned around and quickly barked the orders.

"Go, go, go!"

# CHAPTER SIX

The assault craft were rapidly approaching the planet the troops had so quickly named Red 1. It hadn't required a lot of imagination, but it did catch on fast. They were descending on a new colony with little information or intelligence, a fact that worried them all.

Many of the troops had piled into the 'copters, but they had too few to accommodate the Battalion. Taylor and Chandra were staying aboard the Deveron until they hit the ground. They appreciated their situation, as they knew how much safer they would be. The two officers stood in the hallway entrance leading to the main exterior doorway into the ship. Behind them their troops were packed in close. A projection display on the wall every few metres showed their descent and distance.

The enemy planet was still motionless. It appeared dead by all accounts, but they knew it was a deceptive impression.

"We must have ten thousand soldiers with us," whispered Taylor.

"Thereabouts," replied Chandra.

"Doesn't that strike you as a little odd?"

"How so?"

"Striking out in new territory. Ten thousand soldiers are enough to hopefully have an impact, but few enough that a total loss would not be critical."

She turned and looked in surprise to see Mitch really believed what he was saying. It was a scenario she had not considered.

"And maybe this was just all we could get here. It's a bloody miracle we have a fleet at all. The Deveron is one of the few ships in the fleet built from the beginning as a Navy Vessel. It's bloody remarkable what has been put together."

Mitch knew she could well be right, but he could also hear the hesitation in her voice. He had made her seriously doubt their mission.

"Whatever the intention is, chances are with this mission, it no longer matters. We're here now, so let's do what we were born to do."

They all knew the strategy was doubtful, but they also knew time was not on their side. They could not waste weeks gathering information before making a move. It was all or nothing for the 9th Allied Army, as they had been designated.

"There is no doubt this mission is to test the water and find out if we really can end this in total victory, as we need to," stated Chandra.

Captain Ryan's voice came over the tannoy.

"Landing in three minutes!"

It was the signal for them to pull on their helmets in order to protect themselves from whatever conditions they were entering. It was certain they would fine little or no air to breathe where they were heading. Taylor fell into a daze as the video display of the approaching lands captivated him. The next few minutes passed before he knew it, and he snapped out of it only when he felt the tail of the ship dip as they made their final approach.

"This is it!" called Chandra. "Keep sharp, be ready for anything, and remember all the friends we lost to these bastards!"

Grunts of approval rang out down the line, but it was an odd sensation for many to hate the alien race when two stood among them. For many, they no longer saw Jafar and Tsengal as pure aliens but something in between. They had been humanised to the troops of Inter-Allied, whilst the rest of their race were still the faceless brutal killers they had come to know. Taylor looked around to see if the two of them were put out by Chandra's sentiment, but they were as calm as ever.

The Deveron put down to a smooth and careful

landing, despite the fast pace they had made during their descent. The main door prized opened and lowered to the ground as a ramp. The light bouncing off the red surface flooded into the ship, making them all feel a little sick. They could not smell the air or taste it, but the sight of the alien surface was enough to strike fear into them. None of them had ever stepped foot on a planet other than Earth. Chandra hesitated for a moment, took a deep breath, and jumped forward.

She landed on a dusty rock hard surface and kept moving forward, looking all around with her rifle at the ready. Taylor was quick to follow at her side. Gravity was lighter than on Earth. The two of them were first off the boat, but their 'copters had already put down nearby. The surface was still eerily quiet. Deep caverns were up ahead, and several metallic structures protruded just half a metre above the ground.

Taylor wondered for a moment what they were doing there. They had not surveyed the ground. They had little understanding of what might beneath it. Before he could say a word, the Colonel drove forward towards the nearest structure, and the rest of them followed.

"I want a breach here, now," Chandra ordered through the radios.

Taylor was surprised to hear her voice, as their comms had always been jammed in combat. The demo team leapt forward and laid down magnetic devices that clamped themselves on as they landed.

They all took a knee and awaited the team to do their job. As they waited, they heard another explosion ring out and looked around to see a German infantry unit rush through a breach and vanish below the surface.

"Fire in the hole!"

The explosion rang out, and several metres of the metalwork of the roof were ripped apart.

"Go, go, go!" shouted Chandra.

They rushed forward into the unknown with shields held before them. Taylor's pulse was rushing, and he knew the others with him would be no different. Several of the unit managed to get to the breach ahead of the Colonel. It was likely she wanted to be through first, but light flashed through the breach, and they knew the first through had been hit.

Dust particles created a fog of the breach that only made it more terrifying. As Chandra passed through, she could see the bodies of three of their unit on the ground. Two of them were already dead. She knew she had to keep moving forward and leave the wounded soldier to the medics, as and when they could reach him.

A few pulses smashed into the wall in front of the Colonel, but the troops of Inter-Allied had already begun to overwhelm the enemy with a barrage of fire. Through the chaos, she caught sight of the first enemy that grabbed her attention and fired several aimed shots in quick succession.

Taylor quickly surveyed the scene as all around him lay down fire. They were in what appeared to be some kind of laboratory. Scattered instruments and machinery had little meaning to the Major. The room was thirty metres long by twenty metres wide. The ceilings were only just tall enough for Jafar to stand in who was at his side. The area could be described as nothing but clinical. It seemed that before their entrance nothing was out of place. There had not been a spec of dirt or dust in sight.

"Keep pushing forward!" Chandra ordered.

She looked around to realise that as usual, their comms were now being jammed.

"God damn, this is getting old!"

A pulse smashed into the top of her shield, and the force knocked her off balance and onto her back. She cursed at having been caught unawares and her clumsy tumble. Taylor let his rifle drop onto his sling and hoisted her to her feet. She quickly lifted up her rifle and gestured for the troops at their back to push forward.

"This stone age communication has to be resolved!" she shouted.

"Amen to that," he replied.

She tried to regain her composure as Jones rushed past to join the fight. The troops were lining the room as the bottleneck left much of the Battalion waiting on the surface. Other units were putting down all around them, and they knew they could not expand out beyond the one breach.

"We've got them on the run!" Jones called out.

The speaker on his suit was transmitting just loud enough for Chandra to hear a few metres away. She pushed forward and joined the shuffle of troops trying to squeeze through the doorway of the room. They reached a ramp that was leading them deep below the surface. Jafar reached their side, but he had nothing to say.

"You must have some idea what this place is?" asked Taylor.

The alien shook his head.

"No, we have never experienced this place, but it is certainly not a colony."

"Then what is it?" Chandra asked.

"A research facility by the looks of things," replied Taylor.

Jafar nodded in agreement, but it was obvious he had no better idea than them. There were flashes up ahead, followed by the ripple of gunfire, but the column didn't stop as they rushed down the ramp ten wide. They descended fifty metres and finally evened out into what was apparently a docking facility. Just two ships lay on the deck and were visibly in some state of repair.

The vast underground hangar was large enough for ten ships the size of the Deveron. Crates of ammunition lay stacked at the walls, but there was no sign of life. Chandra signalled for the troops to spread out as they were at last managing to get through the bottleneck.

"An underground hangar, why? What enemy were they guarding from?" asked Chandra.

"The Meteor showers. They are common on all our worlds."

"So you all live underground?" Taylor asked.

"The higher classes, yes. Living on the surface means the weak do not survive."

"No wonder they want Earth. It truly is a paradise compared to this shithole," replied Taylor.

The silence was broken by the crack of several pulses rushing towards them.

"Cover!"

They rushed to any shelter they could find as the fire increased. Chandra and Taylor managed to get behind one of the two enemy ships nearby. They looked around to see that much of their unit were already returning fire with rapid bursts. Taylor peered around the nose of the ship to see several dozen Mechs flooding into the hangar from the opposite side. They were two hundred metres apart. The creatures seemed to come at them without fear, despite the odds.

The initial wave of creatures was cut down within minutes by the volleys of the first two companies who had got inside the hangar. Chandra smiled as she saw them brought to their knees and fired a few shots at one of the wounded creatures to finish it off. Mechs continued to flood into the hangar, but now they were taking cover behind crates and storage canisters. Chandra leaned back around to Taylor.

"Crazy bastards coming at us like that. They must truly believe they are superior."

"We may have the upper hand today, but don't you forget what it was like to face them with fairer numbers."

Chandra sighed. She was enjoying the moment, but it hit home just how uncertain their situation was. They had caught the enemy by surprise, and the skirmish was far removed from the epic battles they had come to know and dread.

Taylor stepped out to the blunt square nose cone of the ship, which lay on its belly, so he could get a better view. The enemy momentum had been broken, but so had theirs. More Mechs poured into the defences up ahead, and neither party wanted to close the open ground they were fighting over.

"We need to gain some ground!" Taylor shouted.

Chandra looked around for any options to make progress. To their right there was another tunnel like they had come from, but flat this time.

"Take Jones' Company that way, and see if you can get around them!"

Taylor was quick on his feet and rushed out in between the fire to reach the Captain's position.

"Follow me Captain!"

Taylor had barely slowed down as he passed Jones, but the Captain was quick to follow. Mitch looked back to see Jafar and Tsengal were close behind and had followed him through the enemy fire, without order or question. Pulses rushed in between the Company as they made a dash for the corridor. Two were struck, but Taylor knew they couldn't afford to stop for anything.

"Come on!"

He burst into the corridor to where he knew they would be safe, but could only hope no threat lay around the corner ahead. He couldn't stop or risk leaving the others out in the line of fire. His rifle was held forward at the ready, as was his shield. Having the shields back brought an immense amount of comfort to their jobs. He took the turn and was relieved to find it empty.

Taylor carried on for ten metres and finally stopping when he was happy they were all inside. Jones was at the head of his Company with the two aliens either side of him.

"Stay close," whispered Taylor.

He went forward once again at a jogging pace. It was enough to cover ground quickly but not too fast to make a racket or rush into danger. The corridor seemed to go on and on. The lighting was red, as on the surface. It tinted everything to the level that they all blended into the architecture. Mitch could see runners in the floor that were parallel. They ran the length of the corridor, but it was the first time he had noticed them. They appeared to be a kind of rail system for transport. He wanted answers but knew it was insignificant in that moment.

They passed several rooms with open doorways but didn't have time to investigate. Up ahead, lay another bend in the corridor, and one Taylor hoped would lead them to the enemy's flank. He took the turn as quickly as the last one, but stopped in horror. Jones and Jafar stumbled into his back. Before them were Mechs as far as they could see.

"Back!" screamed Taylor.

He fired off a quick few shots as the enemy raised their weapons and opened fire. It was clear they were as surprised to see the humans as much as Taylor and his lot were. Mitch just managed to get back around the corner as a brutal wave of enemy fire gushed down the corridor towards them. He slammed his back against the wall and took in a deep breath.

"Fuck!" he yelled.

He looked back around to see the enemy forces were moving steadily forwards to their position.

"Jones, send a runner to the Colonel. Tell her we've met heavy resistance and are staying put. We cannot assist her."

Taylor leaned out around the corner and fired a burst into the first creature his rifle came to bare against. He quickly ducked back. Jones had already relayed the command and sent the message on.

"How many are there?" he asked.

Taylor shook his head.

"No idea, more than I can readily count."

"We can't hold here. They get to this corner and we're goners."

Taylor stopped and thought for just a moment. He looked back down the corridor over the heads of the troops. He could see the tops of entrance doorways to the rooms leading off from the corridor.

"We'll fall back to those doorways. We can at least defend from there and retreat into the rooms if need be."

"And if those rooms are dead ends?"

"I have no doubt they probably are," replied Taylor glumly.

Jones accepted the grim forecast Taylor had given and turned to usher the troops back quickly while they still had time. The Major and Jafar fired several bursts around the corner and followed the others back. The Company scattered into four rooms with entrances fairly close to one another, giving some cover to fire from. Taylor continued into the same room as Jones. He reloaded and stopped just inside the doorway.

"You know we have absolutely no idea how many of those things are out there," Jones said.

Taylor nodded in agreement.

"We could have just flown into the hornets' next, for all

we know," he continued.

Taylor nodded in agreement once again as he looked out down the hallway, anxiously waiting to see the enemy.

"For Christ's sake, Mitch, are we really that disposable that we can just be thrown into the abyss to see what happens?"

Taylor turned and gave all his attention to the Captain.

"After everything we have been through, we are just being tossed away as if we mean nothing?"

"Possibly, but some one had to carry out this mission. Would it be any fairer throwing raw recruits into this mess? Look, this battle has only just begun. They're gonna have to try a damn sight harder to stop us here."

"Last I looked, it was us on the run," Jones answered.

Shots rang out from the troops on the other side of the corridor, and Taylor leaned out to see the first two Mechs entering the hallway tumble to the ground dead. Their comrades continued to push on past their bodies, as if they meant nothing. Taylor had always assumed the aliens simply had no care for their own, but Jafar and Tsengal had drawn all that into doubt.

"Give 'em hell, boys!" Taylor roared.

He lifted his rifle and joined the fight.

"Come on you bastards!" he screamed.

* * *

Chandra peered over the cockpit of the craft she was hiding behind. Its hull was holding off all the enemy fire levelled at her. Parker and her platoon were huddled under the same cover and returning fire whenever they could. Just over a hundred of the Battalion had managed to get into the hangar with her, but many of the others were still held up on the ramp. She could see that no one wanted to move forward across the open ground between them and the enemy.

One of Jones' troops came rushing across the open ground from where they had departed with Taylor, and she could already tell the news was not good. The messenger ducked and weaved through the fire with his shield held in both hands to provide a buffer. Two rounds struck the shield. The second knocked him off balance, and he tumbled in partially behind the cover near Chandra. She leaned over, hauling him across the floor as another pulse landed where his feet had been a second before.

"Thank you, Ma'am, message from the Major. We've hit heavy resistance, and the enemy is moving forward. He cannot support you."

"God damn it!" But her voice could barely be heard over the furious battle raging around them. She peered up from the cover to quickly assess the situation and was met by blinding volleys of light as the Mechs fired relentlessly at their position. Few of the enemy looked for cover, and they confidently stood their ground.

*We can't stay here,* she whispered to herself.

"What was that, Ma'am?"

She leaned in closer so he could hear.

"Get to Captain Jackson, and tell him we are moving forward in two minutes. Be ready to provide support!"

The man's face was pale and his eyes wide with shock.

"You heard me! We're going forward!"

He got to his feet and rushed back towards the ramp. She looked up to see the messenger get to Jackson a minute after leaving. The Captain looked up to find her and met her stare within a few seconds. He quizzed the news with a confused expression, but she responded with a nod. He lifted up his arm and gave a thumbs-up in acceptance.

The Colonel took a deep breath as she looked down at her watch, counting the seconds down. Fifteen seconds from time, she got to her feet and signalled all around her to rise. They could all see what was coming. Most were on their feet but still hunched down to get what cover they could.

"Now!" she shouted.

She held her rifle up high in the air and waved it towards the enemy. It was the only signal they needed. The hundred or more soldiers already in the hangar rose up and drove forwards with their shields held firmly out in front. Jackson rushed ahead, and his troops poured out from the corridor with the cover of the charge.

Chandra leapt out from cover to take her place amongst

the troops as they advanced at a steady pace. She quickly targeted one of the enemy with her rifle held beside the shield, firing on the move. Pulses rushed at them, smashing their shield wall. Their pace was increasing, but they all knew they could only take so much punishment. The intensity of the enemy fire increased, and three of the shields were burnt through under the sustained battering. The rounds pierced the shields and smashed into the soldiers behind them. Chandra saw a few go down around her, but there was nothing she could do but go on.

They advanced forward in a single line because the hangar was so vast, but Jackson's troops were quick to cover the distance, filling the gaps as the wounded were left behind. They were just fifty metres from the enemy now, and they kept up continuous fire on the enemy who stood their ground.

"Keep moving forward! Go!" Chandra shouted.

A pulse smashed into the corner of her shield as she said it, tearing off a piece that clipped the side of her helmet. Fortunately, it didn't break the visor. Before she knew it, they were on top of the enemy. The speed of the Reitech suits was something that still surprised them all. She kept up her pace and rushed in a full sprint at the nearest creature.

The Colonel was just half the size of the creature, even with all her equipment, but her ferocious charge sent the beast tumbling over. Before it could recover, she fired a burst from her rifle into its back. The magazine was out. She dropped the rifle to her side and drew out her Assegai. As she turned to find a new target, her shield was shattered by the impact of a Mech smashing it with its cannon.

Chandra was thrown off her feet like a ragdoll and against the body of another of the enemy creatures. She collapsed down on the floor and was unconscious before she'd landed.

* * *

"Christ!" Taylor yelled, as a pulse smashed into the doorway beside him, and fragments of burning hot metal singed the surface of his helmet.

"Mitch, this is getting fucking hot!" shouted Jones. He was reloading his rifle only a metre away.

Taylor turned to reply but stopped as he heard something bounce on the ground in the corridor. He turned and saw a metal ball almost the size of a football slide to a halt next to them.

"Get down!"

He had barely enough to time to turn and jump with Jones as a massive explosion erupted in the hallway. The blast burst through the entrance and projected them several metres further along. They smashed into the floor hard and slid into a worktop with debris crashing all around them. Taylor shook his head, trying to regain composure but was stunned from the landing.

"Grenades?" asked Jones. "Are you fucking serious?"

"What, you thought we were the only ones with toys?" muttered Taylor.

Their suits had saved them from the deafening blast, but they were still stunned from the shock of the landing.

"Let's give them a taste, then," replied Jones.

He pulled a grenade from his armour and rushed to the entrance. He popped his head out for a second to see where they had gotten to, ducking back as a pulse rushed past his head.

"Christ, they've covered some ground!"

He twisted the firing cap and launched it around the corner, looking for any risk of being hit by the continuous stream of fire.

"Have that, you bastards!"

He ducked down as the explosion rang out down the corridor. Taylor quickly got to his feet and peered around the corner to see a dust cloud and three dead Mechs. He smiled, but energy pulses gushing through the fog-like cloud soon washed his joy away. He jumped back and drew out a grenade, quickly throwing it as Jones had.

A second after the explosion rang out, he was around the corner and firing rapidly. Taylor could not make out a target, but he knew behind the dust lay a wall of Mechs that he couldn't miss. Others of his unit did likewise. They could see the silhouette of two creatures in the smoke be riddled with fire until they dropped, but more continued after them.

"More grenades!" Taylor shouted.

He threw his last one down the corridor and saw several others follow seconds after the blast. Taylor hunkered back inside the room to change his magazine and let Jones take over.

"They're almost on us, Mitch. We've got about thirty seconds!"

The Captain was firing on full auto because they were so close. Taylor looked around to see the platoon they had in the room had taken up defensive positions around the tables and whatever furniture they could find. They waited silently and still. He could see the fear in their pale faces. Their backs were against he wall. They had nowhere to run.

"Jones, come on!"

The two of them rushed back further into the room to take cover. Huge drums as tall as their chests lay in a line that would provide cover, but they had no idea what they contained.

"I bloody hope these things aren't flammable," Jones called out.

"I'll take my chances," replied Taylor.

They readied their weapons and waited with baited breath for the enemy to appear. The corridor had gone quiet. The rest of the Company had retreated as they had done. It was less than a minute before they saw movement.

The sight of the Mechs advancing relentlessly forwards was never something any of them had gotten used to, nor wanted to.

"Fire!"

The opening volley killed the first enemy soldier instantly, and the second fell soon after. The next two got through the doorway but were hit by even more bullets. They could see many of the creatures passing their entrance and moving onto the next. Taylor didn't want to pass them off onto his comrades, but he was glad that some of the pressure was being taken off them.

"Give 'em all you got!"

The gunfire was almost continuous as the Mechs tried to force their way into the room. The doorway was only wide enough for two of the creatures at a time, and their dead were amassing in the bottleneck. It was a turkey shoot, and not one of them felt any sympathy for their opponents. Jafar and Tsengal were with Taylor and showing no mercy against their own kind.

After a few minutes, the bodies of twenty Mechs lay scattered and piled in the entrance, and the next waves were struggling to force through their own dead. Taylor looked down to find a magazine, but out of the corner of his eye caught sight of another enemy grenade bouncing into the room.

"Get down!"

The explosion rocked the barrels, but clearly they

weighed a hell of a lot more than they looked. It sheltered them from the blast. Taylor looked across their line to see shrapnel had hit only one of their own people. He slammed in a new magazine and lifted up once more to continue firing. To his surprise there were no targets.

For a few moments, they all stood silently with their rifles at the ready. None of them could believe the attack was over.

"Have we done it?" asked Jones.

Taylor shrugged his shoulders in surprise. He jumped cautiously over the defences and immediately lifted his rifle to the ready. He walked slowly towards the mound of enemy dead, kicking the nearest to be certain it was dead. Smoke still arose from its armour where grenade fragments had burned through.

Mitch climbed up onto the enemy dead and stumbled through the doorway, having to duck under, due to the pile of bodies. He dropped out into the corridor the other side and looked in amazement to see it was empty.

"Clear!" he called.

Cheers rang out from inside the room as the platoon rushed to join him. He turned and looked to see that the corridor was awash with enemy dead and piled high at each of the doorways.

"We did it," said Jones.

Taylor looked down to see that he was dangerously low on ammunition.

"Form up! The Colonel still needs our help!"

It was a few minutes before the Company was able to fight their way out of the rooms through the bloody mess. He knew they'd taken casualties, but he didn't want to think about it right then.

"Let's move out!"

He quickly got to a steady jogging pace but was sure to keep his shield at the ready, should he meet another enemy force. A few moments later, he caught sight of familiar faces up ahead, realising the rest of the Battalion had successfully fought their way across the hangar.

"Friendlies incoming!"

He rushed through the lines to see enemy and human dead scattered among each other. Several soldiers were gathered around one of the wounded, and Taylor rushed up to see that it was the Colonel. He pushed one of them aside and knelt down beside her. She was propped up against the armour of a fallen Mech. She looked stunned and weak, but still alive.

"You okay?"

"Just about."

"Can you walk?"

She looked away, finally looking back and almost in tears.

"I'm not sure I want to find out."

Taylor looked back to see the medics busily working with other wounded.

"You! Help the Colonel!"

"No!" she cried.

"Can you move your legs?" he asked.

"She looked down at them and tried. Very slowly, they shifted a little."

"Jesus, you're okay!"

To her surprise, Taylor grabbed her and hauled her up to her feet. It was against everything he had ever learnt about injuries, but he knew it was all or nothing in that moment. She wobbled a little but managed to stay upright.

"I've taken worse beatings."

Taylor sighed in relief. He suddenly realised how stupid it was to have pulled her up after potential injuries, but he was glad she was okay. He looked around to see the bodies of over fifty Mechs and twenty of their own scattered along the deck. Several of their wounded had their helmets off, to his surprise.

"We can breathe down here?"

"For up to an hour or more, yes. The mixture isn't quite what we're used to and could cause us problems in prolonged periods," she replied.

Taylor ripped off the fully enclosed helmet, which he'd always found claustrophobic, and took in a deep breath. The air was thick with the smell of burning metal and sweat, but it was still appreciated. Taylor was about to settle down on a nearby crate when a loud mechanical cranking sound echoed around the huge hangar. He leapt back up to his feet and held his rifle at the ready. The rest of them froze and looked around for the source.

They quickly realised a massive shutter was opening a hundred metres away from their position.

"What the hell is this?" asked Taylor.

"Take up positions!" Chandra ordered.

They settled into what cover they could find as the shutter came to a halt. The opening it left was fifteen metres high and a similar width. They half expected to see a horde of Mechs stomp out, but they had no such luck. To their horror, a huge robotic leg stepped out into the light, and the rest of a ten metre-tall Mech followed it.

"Oh, my God," muttered Taylor.

The creature resembled an enlarged version of the Mechs they had so recently fought, but it was vast, and like a tank on legs. It moved slowly, in fitting with the mammoth size. It finally cleared the entrance and turned to face them. Artillery size cannons festooned its arms, and the armour looked thicker than any vehicle they'd encountered. It looked unfinished, partially built, but still operational to scare the life out of the most steadfast of them.

*Oh, shit,* thought Taylor.

The Colonel wasn't willing to wait to learn anymore.

"Fire!"

A hundred rounds struck the monster, but they seemed to have little effect. Lights beamed from it as pulses rushed towards them. It raised one of its arms and fired from the four-metre long gun barrel running down its forearm. The blast landed ten metres from Taylor, yet tossed him aside as if he was nothing. He looked back to see five dead, including one of their medics. Chandra was crawling for cover.

Hundreds of rounds were pouring into the massive metallic beast, but it continued to rain down hell on them all. Taylor looked to see that many were running for cover and hunkering down from the ferocious onslaught.

"Christ! Mines, Mines! Do we have any?"

"We've still got a few mag charges!" Corporal Hall shouted.

The charges had been their way into the facility earlier that day, and it was the only thing Taylor could think of. He gestured for them to be passed to him. A box was slid across the surface to him, and he opened it to see just one of the devices.

"Fuck it!"

He turned to see four others, including Corporal Hall, had got the devices ready to follow after him. He knew it was suicidal, but they were being butchered.

Taylor leapt out from cover and was joined by the other four volunteers. The five of them darted forward to the next line of cover as quickly as they could. He hunkered down and turned back to them.

"We're only gonna get one chance each at this, so make

it count. Aim for the legs or head!"

They looked up to see that the monster didn't really have a head. Like the Mechs themselves, it had a mirrored plate section where the head would normally be, and the shoulder line rose above it.

"It's probably controlled by one of the bastards. That's where he'll be. Head or legs."

"Could we throw these things?" asked Hall.

"No, it's too risky. This is the only chance we're gonna get. It's all or nothing, you ready?"

He could see the fear in the Corporal's eyes, and yet he was still willing to go forward. They could see there was little to no cover left between them and the massive Mech.

"Cover the ground as quickly as you can, get the device planted, and get out! Now go!"

They rushed out from the cover, and two of the soldiers erupted in a flash of light before they'd even got up a pace. Hall was at the front, Taylor at the rear of the three. They were spread several metres apart. The quick pace allowed them to cover the ground quickly, but pulses still exploded all around them. The man between him and Hall vanished into a fireball that Taylor had to rush through and hope for the best. The heat singed his hair, and he'd wished he had kept his helmet on.

Taylor saw Hall sprint for the legs and slap the device onto the creature as he rushed past. The creature swung down its arm to strike him, but he was already sprinting fast enough to steam past. This was Taylor's opportunity. Hall running beneath it distracted the creature. He used the power of his suit to launch him into the air to the full height of the creature.

As he flew through the air, he realised how insane his plan had been, but he was already long past the point of no return. He tumbled into the faceplate of the beast and only held on as the magnetic explosive device clamped on. The beast immediately responded by trying to reach up to Taylor, but its arms couldn't reach. Taylor lifted himself and jumped up onto the shoulders of the creature.

He knew he had only a few seconds to spare. Mitch looked up to see the support structure of the hangar twenty metres above. He leapt up and used his boosters to reach it, clinging onto the supports for sheer life. A second later an explosion ripped out below him. He looked down to see the giant Mech begin to fall slowly like timber. As it struck the surface of the hangar, a second explosion ripped through its armour, sending shrapnel soaring across into the far wall. Taylor gave out a sigh of relief. He released his grip and let his suit bring him to a soft landing in the rubble.

Taylor smiled as he stood triumphantly among the wreckage of their vanquished foe. Hall strode up to him with a look of pure shock and awe.

"We fucking did it," he whispered.

"Hell, yeah!"

# CHAPTER SEVEN

General White stepped through the ruins of the vast armoured creature with a look of horror on his face. Chandra was still being checked over by the medics, and Taylor was overseeing the resupply of the Battalion. White was lost for words. Captain Jones walked up to the Major with a grim expression. It was the news Taylor didn't want to hear.

"Final total, Sir. Twenty-six wounded, thirty-five dead."

Taylor nodded, but it made him just as sick as such news always had. The General had heard, and it had finally forced him to speak.

"That was damn fine work here, Taylor. In the face of such horror, you prevailed."

"Thank you, Sir."

Mitch gestured for their two alien allies to step up and join them.

"This place, what does it mean to you? What can you tell us about it?" he asked.

"So much of what is here we have never seen before," replied Jafar. "It looks like a testing ground for new technology."

"An experimental base?" asked White.

"If this had been a primary colony, we would not have taken it with ten thousand men," replied Tsengal.

*That's reassuring,* thought Taylor. *We survived because of the luck of the draw.*

"We've had a couple of years of reverse engineering and development under our belt. Clearly, they haven't been sat idly by either," stated White.

"This monster, this Goliath, could very nearly have been the end of our entire Battalion. Just like that," replied Taylor, clicking his fingers.

It was a frightful thought, and he still could not believe he'd survived the ordeal.

"What do we do now, Sir?"

"We aren't setting up home here, Major, that's for sure. But we are going to hold here for a while. I want to know everything we can about this place, and if we can justify pushing on into the system."

"That would not be advisable, Sir," replied Jafar quickly.

White snapped around and stared into the eyes of the towering alien.

"Explain it to me."

"The Krycenaean people are strong. We are too few."

"We?" White asked in surprise.

He looked down at the creature's uniform, not unlike his own, at least in insignia and colour.

"You believe we need a lot more soldiers to continue this war?"

Jafar nodded quickly in return.

"I agree, but convincing the appropriate authorities is no easy task. They will need to hear as such from someone they will believe."

"They need to hear it from you, Sir," Taylor added.

The General sighed and shook his head. He knew it to be true. He stepped past Taylor and stood before Chandra. She was still in pain.

"Colonel Chandra, I am leaving you in command of all operations on Red 1. I need troops who can fight, and yet I must go and plead for them with ignorant politicians."

"We all have our battles to fight," she answered.

"Indeed. I will return in four weeks. With any luck, at the head of the army we need."

"Did we not muster every ship we could for this fleet?" asked Taylor.

"There are still plenty of civilian transports that could carry tens or hundreds of thousands of troops into combat. I want to take this war to their soil and spill their blood over it."

"And if we are attacked in your absence?"

"You are to hold as long as is realistic, Colonel. Should the fleet be endangered, Admiral Huber has been ordered to return home.

The General turned and rushed away to his shuttle. Taylor was still curious as to how surprised Jafar and Tsengal were to behold one of their own planets.

"Experimental planet?" asked Taylor. "I bet Reiter could have a few things to say and learn about this place. I want him and his team down here asap."

Chandra nodded in agreement.

"Make it happen."

They'd been on the enemy planet for less than half a day, and the General was already departing for Earth. Taylor was well aware of the bureaucracy and still hated it as much as ever. He turned to see that Chandra had laid down flat on her back. She was both exhausted and physically weak.

"You're gonna have to handle things for a day or two," she said as he stood over her.

"No problem."

It took several days before they fully understood how the docking hangar worked and allowed the Deveron and many other ships to land on Red 1. The ships were a welcome home for the troops stationed there. Reiter was clearly fascinated by so much of what he saw, but it was clear to Taylor that anything learned would not assist them anytime soon. On the third day of their occupation,

Chandra returned to full duty.

The bridge of the Deveron had become their office and command post. The enemy had only a few thousand troops on Red 1 that had fallen within a day. Taylor could not help but feel what power the enemy might hold if they brought their population to bare against the humans. No matter how he asked Jafar and Tsengal about the aliens' population, they seemed to have little idea on numbers.

For the troops of Inter-Allied, their time on Red 1 was nothing more than another posting. They had seen enough of the enemy for a lifetime, and anything that could be learned there was not for them. On the morning of the fourth day, Taylor strolled out onto the surface in gear to marvel at the alien planet.

It was an ugly place with no redeeming features. He wondered how life could ever have been supported there, or why anyone would choose to live there. Yet he thought back to Commander Kelly and his love of his homeland, despite similarly inhospitable characteristics. Huber's fleet still waited in orbit, and it was a reassuring sight. Taylor thought he was alone and went into a daze as he stared out across the barren surface.

Time seemed a glide by as he fell into a dream. A hand grasped his shoulder, and he turned quickly to see Parker standing with him.

"What do you see in it?" she asked.

"I'm not sure I see anything. Look at it, what's to like?"

He wanted nothing more than to kiss her, but their suits made it impossible. He settled for grasping her hand and looking out to the fleet. Their engines suddenly fired up, and they began to move off from the planet.

"What the hell?"

Taylor turned and rushed back inside. He tried to contact the Deveron, but their channel was busy. He rushed on board to find Chandra awaiting him.

"Huber's leaving?"

"We have picked up readings of enemy ships in the area and even a few sightings by recon parties. The Admiral is returning to the gateway to ensure its safety."

"And us? What about our safety?"

They had just over two thousand troops on the now desolate enemy colony.

"We can look after ourselves. Follow me."

Taylor was surprised she shrugged off the situation so lightly but did as she asked. The Colonel led him deeper into the colony to a floor he'd never been to. They came to huge blast doors.

"What are we doing?"

She tapped a few buttons, and a section of wall became transparent. He looked in with horror to see over a hundred Mechs in various states of injury.

"The survivors from our assault."

"Survivors?" asked Taylor.

Chandra nodded.

"They always seem to take their wounded away, but here they had nowhere to run. We believe that many committed suicide when they had nowhere left to go, mostly by charging our guns. These are what's left."

Most of the creatures were in various degrees of armour and lay on the metal floor. Blood stained much of the visible surface in the room. It reminded him of the human bodies stacked high in the prison where they had rescued Jones so long ago. The feeling made him sick to his stomach.

"What are we to do with them? Reiter thinks we could learn a lot," she asked.

"Learn a lot?" Taylor asked in disgust.

"We don't keep prisoners in this war," she replied.

"Is that what we have become? Is it genocide we want, just as they did?"

Taylor turned away at the horrific sight.

"We must make a decision. We have little idea what to do with them. We can't send them packing."

Taylor remained silent for a moment, and then whispered.

"Put them out of their misery."

"What was that?"

"You heard me. End their miserable lives."

She was surprised to hear him say the words after taking on two of their kind as friends. She lifted her comms unit and spoke into it.

"Captain Jackson, you have a green light."

Taylor turned just in time to see a large door open within the chamber and thirty of the Captain's Company enter, guns blazing. They executed the creatures where they lay. Taylor watched for several minutes until the room was silent.

"Is this what it has come to? Must it end with the complete destruction of one of our races?"

She nodded yes. "Afraid so."

Taylor turned and strode away. He had seen enough. He wasn't sure the Colonel was wrong, but it made him sick to see it done, either way. Another two days passed without event until on the third, a message came over the intercom for Taylor to make his way to the bridge. It was early in the morning, and the Major still thought about the mass execution he had witnessed. He found the Colonel on the bridge, waiting to address him personally.

"Admiral Huber has asked that Inter-Allied return to the fleet in defence of the Washington."

"What of this planet?"

"General White left me in charge here, and that is exactly where I will remain. You will return to the Washington with the Battalion while I remain in command of all ground forces here."

"You'll have what, less than three thousand troops?"

"This planet means something to our enemy, perhaps much more than we realise. I want to know what it is, and

I will not give it back to them without a fight."

"Then let us stay. Let us fight this together."

"I am sorry, Major, but we all have our orders. The protection of the Washington is paramount, and I would trust no other to carry out such a task. You will return to the fleet immediately."

"Will you at least take some of our own in support?"

She conceded to his advice.

"Suarez and his platoon will remain as a personal detail to myself. I would keep Tsengal, if I could. He may yet provide insight into what we have found here."

"He is under your command, Colonel, not mine."

"Then it is agreed. Get moving Major."

She strode off the bridge to leave the ship and allow them to prepare for departure.

*Suarez? You hate the bastard, and yet you're keeping him at your side?* He thought.

Taylor didn't like it one bit, but he had no choice but to go along with the commands. Ever since the execution of the prisoners, his relationship with the Colonel had been modified. He knew she had done the only thing she could. He also knew she had in fact saved them from invasive research, which they would not wish on any soldier. He wanted to tell her he had her back, but the time and words did not come.

"Put out the word, Captain, Inter-Allied is to report here for departure in one hour."

Captain Ryan didn't look happy about the orders either, but there was nothing either of them could do. The hour passed quickly, and a few minutes before final preparations, the Colonel reappeared to say her goodbye. Taylor was glad to see her once more before they left. He hated leaving things in a bad way with one of his closest friends. He saluted her as she approached.

"The enemy are amassing. I'd say we have about a day before anything kicks off," she said.

"And you really think this is a good time for us to be leaving?"

"The Washington must be protected, and they'll be coming for the gateway. I still think this planet has a lot to tell us that we have not yet seen. Orders are to hold it, and that order was given to me. We all have our duties."

"You know if the fleet gets into trouble, it can bug out through the gate. What are you going to do?"

She smiled in response.

"I'll give them hell. I'll make them remember why they don't mess with the human race. Our leaders need to know what they face. They need to understand what it at stake, and they must be willing to do what is necessary."

She looked down at her watch.

"Time for you to go. You look after the fleet, you hear? There will come a time when it is needed, probably more than you know. The day we can destroy the enemy before they reach our colonies, that is a great day."

Taylor knew there was nothing more he could say to change the situation. They were leaving for the fleet and leaving so few behind. He could see in her eyes that she was fearless. She didn't want to die. She only wanted the best for them all.

"Tsengal, you have kept to your word and been a valuable asset to me and the unit. I would ask you now protect the Colonel, as you have done me."

"I will."

Taylor noticed Suarez stood behind the Colonel. He had a triumphant and sleazy grin on his face that unsettled Taylor. Mitch disliked the fact the man served under him. He didn't trust the Lieutenant among his friends, but he had no choice. The Colonel's word was final. He saluted her and turned to make his way aboard the Deveron. He turned back just at the doorway.

"You look after yourself, Colonel."

She smiled in return as he made his way aboard. When he reached the bridge, he could see she had already left to continue her investigation into the enemy world. She had been fixated on their technology since the moment they stepped foot there. But he'd never cared for any of it.

"When you're ready, Captain."

Leaving the enemy world was a welcome thing to Taylor, but he knew home was still far from sight. As they ascended from the planet, he could see half a dozen other ships heading the same way.

"Huber must be pretty concerned about the risk of attack."

He was fishing for information, but it was clear Ryan didn't have it.

"Wouldn't you be, Sir? The Navy's most powerful ship moored up in enemy territory, and light years from home. I am surprised the Colonel has not left Red 1 and come with us."

"She is making a statement."

"How so, Sir?"

"Throughout the war, we spent most of our time running, giving ground. This mission proved we could go forward and take land. She isn't going to give it up without a fight."

Ryan went silent. They both knew it was a dangerous game she was playing, but it was not for them to say. Taylor speculated she must have well under three thousand troops with her. The doors of the bridge slid open, and Captain Jones walked quickly through with purpose.

"We're leaving?"

"On the Admiral's orders," replied Taylor.

"And she stayed, didn't she?"

Taylor nodded. "We all have our duties."

"We must petition the Admiral to move at least some of our forces from the gateway to protect what we have already taken."

"Damn right, we'll do everything we can."

\* \* \*

It was another day before Huber's fleet came into sight. The space gateway they were guarding like gatekeepers dwarfed the two vast carriers. It was a sight to behold and marvel at, but Taylor could only wish he were back home on solid ground. The Deveron docked once again with the Washington to deliver its payload of marines. Taylor headed right for the bridge.

He remembered the carrier well and was already familiar with navigating it. As he passed through corridors he had fought in just weeks before, he could still see much of the superficial damage. He stepped aboard the bridge alone and was greeted by the Admiral.

"I see she still shows the scars of battle."

"We're back to full operating condition, but those scars are a bitter reminder of what could have been. I wouldn't want any of my crew to forget what threats we face."

"I couldn't agree more, Sir. May we speak privately?"

The Admiral turned and led Taylor away into his quarters. They both knew there was a lot to discuss, and that none of it should be done privately. The door shut behind the two of them, and Taylor jumped in before the Admiral had even managed to sit down.

"Sir, what are we doing here? We've left our commanding officer out on her ass when we both know trouble is on its way."

"Colonel Chandra is free to leave Red 1 and return to the fleet whenever she pleases. However, General White ordered her to hold there as long as she can. I cannot order her to do otherwise."

"But you can help her. If the colony is attacked, she'll need more troops, supplies and air support."

"I am sorry, Major, but I will not divide our forces. I cannot commit the whole fleet. I cannot risk leaving Earth exposed through this gate."

"So what are we to do, sit here until trouble comes our way?"

Huber sat down with a sigh and pulled out a bottle of whiskey, letting Taylor calm down.

"My orders were to hold this position and take a single enemy position if possible. The honest truth is nobody knew what we would find. We have what, ten thousand troops among us? It's not enough to hold a colony, nor expand any further. General White has returned with news of our victory. He should return with armies in number great enough to continue into the system."

"And if we can't hold out that long?"

"Then we will return to Earth, knowing that this was an unrealistic enterprise and that we overstretched ourselves."

"Meanwhile we've still got a few thousand troops on that planet."

"They've got their own transport."

Taylor was kicking himself inside. He knew how

stubborn Chandra could be. He wanted nothing more than to get back on the Deveron and return to Red 1, but it was no longer in his hands.

"Earth's armies were preparing for this eventuality, Major. We should see reinforcement within a few weeks. Your presence here is reassuring to my crew. You really saved our asses. I suggest you get some rest."

It wasn't what Taylor wanted to hear, but he knew there was no arguing with it. There was nothing more to do with himself. It was already evening and watches had been set. He resigned himself to a few drinks in the NAAFI. Jones had beaten him to it. He could see the Captain was even more frustrated by the situation than he was. Mitch took a seat next to him without a word.

"The Colonel, she had those prisoners killed, didn't she?" he asked.

Taylor glanced in shock. He'd assumed she had kept it secret, particularly after Jones' time as a prisoner of the creatures.

"It's okay. I knew. She told me. I just didn't want you to think we had any secrets."

Taylor shook his head as he knocked back a drink.

"It was the right thing to do, you know," Jones carried on.

Taylor was taken aback.

"It was the kindest thing to do. Kept alive, they'd be lab rats for scientists. They'd be poked, prodded, injected with poisons and experimented on, like they did to us."

"And you don't think we could have taken prisoners?"

"Maybe someday, but not now. This is a war of uncertainty. Chandra, she showed pity on them and ended their misery."

Taylor thought Jones had finally overcome his ordeal, but it was clear it still weighed heavily on him.

*Perhaps he is right.* Taylor thought.

He remembered the squalid and disgusting conditions he had found Jones in so long ago, and imagined what it could have been like.

*Would it have been kinder to have been killed there and then, when he was captured? Maybe, but then Jones wouldn't be here today.*

"You think General White will return with the armies we need?" asked Jones.

"How'd you know that's what he is doing?"

"Oh, come on. This is total war, not a few skirmishes. We all know this opening operation was just a test. The real fighting is yet to come."

"We should have just destroyed the gateway and be done with it," muttered Taylor.

"They said it couldn't be done?"

"Bullshit. I know Reiter, and he could have found a way. They don't want that gateway destroyed because they see opportunity; politicians and desk jockeys who don't ever have to carry a rifle and bleed and die to pursue their goals."

"You really believe that to be the case? You think Earth leaders would risk it all?"

"Of course. Curiosity has got the better of them, and we have to pay the price for that. This war is long from over, years from being over. They say we won the first war, but the truth is it never ended. While that gateway remains, and both our civilisations exist, there can be no peace."

"I thought I was the cynical one. You've made two friends from their race. Why not more?" replied Jones.

"Don't get me wrong. I am glad to have them, but I think we are a world away from convincing any others to join us. And even if you could, they would never be trusted. Jafar and Tsengal have enough trouble as it is, and they proved themselves to me personally. No, I think that is a unique situation which we will not see repeated anytime soon."

"Is there no way you could convince the powers that be to close the gateway for good?"

Taylor shook his head and rolled it around. His neck was stiff; he was aching from inactivity.

"Maybe there is a chance if we ever get back home, but what am I? Just a combat officer, not an adviser to Command, or to the President, or to world leaders."

"No, but you hold more power than you believe. That statue in Paris, it's of you, you defeating Karadag. It is you people think of when they remember the soldiers who won this war."

"Soldier? I'll be a marine for as long as I live."

"You know what I'm saying. People know your face, and they will listen to what you have to say."

If indeed Jones was right, Taylor knew it was an immense amount of responsibility being placed on his shoulders to act in ways he had no experience of.

"I will do everything I can when we return home."

"And you think that will be anytime soon?"

"We either lose here and run for home, or we win and the problem is no longer apparent."

Jones breathed out a weary sigh.

"You're just a paragon of positivity this evening."

The next day they sat around the operations table as they listened to a live report being given by Chandra from Red 1. The distance between them caused a delay in the signal of almost ten seconds, but it was small enough to still communicate live. She stood next to a block of cylinders standing twenty metres high.

"Reiter says this is where the air is coming from. They somehow generate a mix not so different to what we have on earth. They are drawing it from ice lakes far beneath the surface. In fact, they pump enough into the atmosphere to make it tolerable in short doses. He now believes that within the confines of the colony, we should be able to breathe for prolonged periods without concern."

"What do you define by prolonged periods?"

"Years of breathing this in to cause a problem," she replied.

Huber rubbed his chin as they all thought about what they were seeing and hearing.

"At every turn the creatures seem more and more like us," Taylor said.

"Yes. We have also found an interesting few pieces of technology that we have not seen before, on top of the Goliath we encountered. I want to send Doctor Reiter back to the fleet with his findings, so he can continue his work in a safer environment."

"Affirmative, Colonel. He is more than welcome back aboard the Washington."

"I'll have him on his way within a day."

"Have you any recent sightings of the enemy?" asked Huber.

"None, Sir, but we are ready and prepared for them, should they try and retake the colony."

"Good work, Colonel."

"Sir, I have to ask. It seems we're being left out here as bait. General White has returned to Earth. What are his and your intentions?"

Taylor smiled that she didn't pull any punches, yet remained polite whilst doing so.

"You know as much as I, Colonel. I believe, based on our success, we will be reinforced within a few weeks. At such time, we will continue into enemy territory. Any more questions?"

"No, Sir."

"Keep us up-to-date with any finds, Huber out."

The transmission cut off, and the Admiral turned to Taylor.

"You see, Taylor. She's doing just fine. A damn fine officer that one."

Taylor knew he had no choice but to settle back into normal life on the Washington. They were light years away from home, and yet were being order to lay idle as if there was no war.

"Sir, what kind of recon and fleet protection details are you currently running?"

"We have scouts out five ten kilometres in all directions. Fighters are on two-hour flybys. We're ready for anything. I hope you will be to."

"Yes, Sir."

Taylor didn't let up on his guard duties and drills. He had eight hundred under his command, with those of Inter-Allied and the ship's own marines. They might as well all be marines, considering their recent posting. The more he navigated the carrier and carried out drills, the more he realised it was simply not enough in the event of a major boarding action.

The ship's crew would have to become combat ready in the event of such an attack, but he knew they lacked much of the equipment. They had spare Reitech weapons and ammo, but without the exoskeleton suits, they had to be treated as heavy weapons on mounts and tripods. It was better than nothing but far from ideal. He had several Navy heavy weapon teams stationed around the bridge on a permanent basis. The design of the ship had made them all believe the Command Centre was safe from all but catastrophic failure or destruction of the ship, but recent events had proven otherwise.

When they left Earth, the fleet felt invincible. Their quick victory had only fed the ego of the crew, and that worried Taylor more than anything. Huber understood the risks and knew they just got by in their first battle, but he couldn't bring himself to sour the morale of the fleet by pointing it out.

Taylor prowled the corridors of the ship, expecting to find an enemy intruder at any moment. His attitude amused many aboard, who arrogantly believed they were superior to their enemy. Taylor knew a battle was coming. He knew it would be brutal, and he knew there was nothing more he could do about it.

# CHAPTER EIGHT

Chandra stood by a drone they'd become accustomed to seeing in combat with the enemy. It was partially disassembled and parts she had not seen before lay nearby. Tools and component lay everywhere, as well as a storage room filled with another dozen inactive pieces.

"Looks like they were trying to modify and upgrade," she said to Tsengal.

"Yes, I have not seen some of these components."

"This whole planet seems to be devoted to the development of weapons. It's not what I'd expected to find."

Tsengal looked at her as if to ask why but did not speak.

"Throughout this entire war, we have been researching and evolving our equipment, more so in two years than the last two hundred. I just didn't expect to find them doing the same."

"Our former leaders underestimated the humans. A mistake they are rapidly trying to correct, by the looks."

"Back on Earth, we found scores of humans, or what looked like humans in some kind of incubation chambers. Do you know anything of them?"

He shook his head.

"I am sorry, Colonel."

A transmission came in to her personal comms link.

"Colonel Chandra. Colonel Chen is requested your presence at the CP immediately."

Her curiosity turned to concern. She had been waiting for bad news for days.

"Come on let's go!"

She took to a running pace. Several of the troops they passed on the way turned in surprise and reached for their weapons. They could all see it was serious, and yet even she didn't yet know the reason for such an emergency. The two of them rushed into the Command centre that they had established in what seemed to be the docking bay control room.

Passing through the guards and the entrance, the Colonel could already see the worry in the faces of those waiting for her. The three Battalion commanders were all gathered around a table that had a map of their area displayed. She rushed up to them without a word, looking to Colonel Chen for answers.

"We have confirmed sightings of the enemy, Ma'am."

"What's their strength?"

"Unknown, but it's not small. They're coming right for us. At their current speed, we have about eight hours until they arrive."

"We should prepare our defences," Major Warren added.

Chandra nodded in agreement. The Commando officer was thinking exactly as she did.

"We've got what, less than three thousand troops? Enough to hold off a scouting party or small assault, maybe more with the terrain here. But if they come at us hard, like we have seen so many times..." continued Chen.

Major Klimenko's fist smashed down on the table like iron. It made them all jump in shock. The Russian marine stood taller than everyone in the room, except for Tsengal, and his cold fearless expression spoke a thousand words.

"The time for giving up ground is over!" he boomed. "We will spill their blood on their land."

Chen shook his head in disbelief.

"How can you..." he continued.

"Enough!" Chandra shouted. "We came here to fight, so I don't want to hear any talk of bugging out. We have no idea what we are dealing with yet. We have a strong position here, with enough troops to defend it."

The room went silent as Chen swallowed his words.

"There may come a time when we have to turn tail and run, but that is the very last resort. We've been ordered to defend this colony, and we will do so until we are no longer able."

"Suicide? That's what you are asking of us?" asked Chen.

Chandra took a deep breath. She knew Chen was a good man and a solid officer. She didn't want to insult him.

"You fought hard to save the Moon Colony, against all odds. That battle assisted all of us on Earth. As important as that fight was, so could this one be. If we do not stand in the face of the enemy, who will?"

Chen accepted her words, as he knew there was no chance of changing her mind.

"At least request assistance from the fleet," he pleaded.

"I will do so, but no matter their answer, our task is set. I know the breaches we made here have already been sealed, but I'd like them checked and reinforced if need be. You all have your areas marked out. I'll attach myself to Major Warren's commandos for now. You have a good few hours. Let's make this as defensible as we possibly can."

They turned and left. Chandra stood her ground and continued to survey the map of the colony. She could see they had more than enough troops to defend the confined underground facility. She turned to her comms operator.

"Get the Admiral for me."

* * *

Taylor had been called to the bridge. He knew it must be important. The Admiral was well aware he was partaking in hull breach drills and defence practices. He didn't like being interrupted when he was running such drills, as they could mean life or death for many of them. He stepped onto the bridge with a scowl, but it was quickly wiped from his face with a few simple words from Huber.

"Colonel Chandra in on the link."

He quickly stepped up to the briefing table where a projection displayed a video feed.

"Please carry on, Colonel," Huber ordered.

"As I was saying, Sir, we have confirmed enemy incoming in unknown but large number."

"Are they heading for you or us?" asked Taylor.

"Hard to say as their path runs towards you, but we're right in the middle, so you can bet your arse they're going to want this place back."

"We should reinforce Red 1, Sir," insisted Taylor to Huber.

Huber thought about it for a few seconds before directing his question to Chandra.

"What is your analysis of the situation, Colonel?"

"Sir, we have enough strength to effectively defend this colony against a sizeable attack. It is my belief that we should make all efforts to defend this place. If the enemy are heading for the gateway, then they are heading for Earth. The longer we can hold them back, the better prepared our colonies will be."

"You think a few hours or days could make a difference to that?" he asked.

"In the past, I would have said no, but our production, recruitment and training is at an all time high. Every day Earth gains to develop its strength could be vital in determining the outcome of a second invasion."

Taylor could see Huber already agreed with her. They had all witnessed the vast shipyards slaving away and putting new ships into space, in what seemed like a daily basis.

"I will not order you to stay on Red 1, Colonel, but I do believe staying there is the right decision. As you know, we cannot quickly assist you, and if the fleet comes under attack, we may well be unable to provide any extra help."

"Understood, Sir."

"Request for Inter-Allied to return to assist the Colonel, Sir," Taylor asked.

*I know it's a long shot, but I had to ask.*

"Denied, we need the best we have here on the the Washington, to protect us in the event of another breach."

"We'll be fine here, Mitch. I've got some of the very finest troops at my disposal. We bled for this land. I'm not willing to give it up without a fight."

Taylor nodded in agreement. He was well used to the

Colonel's stubbornness.

"You look after yourself."

"Always."

"Good luck, Colonel," Huber added.

"And to you, Sir."

The projection stopped, and Taylor was once more struck by the realisation he was again divided from friends.

* * *

Time flew by on Red 1 as the troops hastened to prepare the defences. Enough hours had passed, and they now waited for the inevitable attack. Chandra sat in the CP with just five other personnel. All the other officers were stationed at their designated zones. Her platoon waited at the door for her.

All were silent as she waited for some news from the staff sat at their stations. She sat upright and sternly, with a straight back. Her rifle lay on the table next to her. They had no planetary defence batteries or fighters to engage the enemy. All they could do was wait for the enemy to come to them. Her comms operator, Corporal Bradley waited anxiously for information more than any of them.

"Ma'am, we have identified forty vessels so far."

She nodded in response.

They had little idea of the enemy strength based on that information, other than it was more than a mere scouting party.

"Transmit all information to the fleet live while you still can."

She could see the fear in the operator's face. It was a gloomy outlook to be trapped in a siege.

"Don't worry, this is only the beginning. They're going to wish they'd never met the human race."

She was trying her best to boost all their morale, but she wasn't sure they believed her. She had the opportunity to smash an enemy army on their own soil, and yet she could not get the support she wanted or needed to do the job properly.

*Why will they not commit the fleet?*

She knew defending the gateway was important, but taking the fight to the enemy would have protected it also, or at least she believed so.

"They have passed within five kilometres, Ma'am."

"And they have not fired?"

The man shook his head.

*Why? They must know we now occupy this place, so why would they not shell the colony? What is so important about it?*

Ever since she had arrived on the planet, she had felt there was more to learn there than they had seen or found so far. The waiting game was a dreadful experience for them all. Finally, the comms operator spoke again.

"Incoming craft landing on the surface."

"Still not a single shot fired? No bombs dropped?"

"No, Ma'am."

"Then our odds just improved. They want this colony badly enough to not risk its destruction. That's the first bit of good news I've heard all day."

He could see what she was saying, but it was little relief when the wolves were at their door.

"We've lost all communications. Hard lines only now, Ma'am."

She had given strict orders that all breaches were to be reported on the hard lines or with runners. The Colonel knew they had a good chance of holding when their lines stayed firm. Any breach must be filled quickly, or they could be overrun. Bradley now sat in front of a board of lights indicating an incoming communication along the wired lines they had set up. It was an antiquated and painfully tedious way of working, but it was the best they could do.

An explosion erupted far from them, and they could just about hear it echo through the corridors. They waited with bated breath for news, and it wasn't long before one of the incoming call lights was flashing. Bradley opened a channel, outputting on the speakers so they could all hear.

"We've got a breach in grid 6B. Enemy contact."

Chandra looked down at the map they had hastily put together of the colony layout, and the positions she had designated for them all. It was Major Warren's area. She wanted to rush out and help, but she knew she must wait for more news. Two other lights quickly flashed on the console, and Chandra could feel her pulse race as each of them lit up.

Within two minutes, they had five breaches in the colony's perimeter, and all three Battalions were reporting enemy contact. She knew it was time to join the fight. They needed all the fighters they could get. She grasped her rifle from the table and rushed to the exit of the room. Stopping at the doorway, she turned back to Bradley and the others for just a moment.

"Have your weapons ready. We're in for a hell of a fight."

It wasn't much relief to any of them, but at least they would be prepared. Suarez and Tsengal were waiting for her with the rest of the platoon. They looked raring to go and eager to draw enemy blood.

"Come on!" she yelled.

They took to a jogging pace and headed for Warren's position. It was the site of the first breach and was therefore the priority. It took just a couple of minutes to reach the back of the Battalion. The small colony allowed them to pack in tight and concentrate their fire. The gunfire they could hear was controlled and steady. Chandra pushed her way through the lines, until finally she reached the front where Warren was overseeing the action.

The defences had been built tall, and she could not see over the barricades what the lines of commandos were firing at. They all seemed remarkably calm, and there were no casualties in sight. The three-dozen rifles firing were evidently holding back whatever was coming at them down the broad hallway.

"Give me an update, Major!" she shouted over the echoing shots.

"Enemy advance has been halted here. We have sustained no casualties."

"Damn good work."

"They're being funnelled in through the breach in so few enough numbers that they aren't making any headway at present."

Chandra was glad to hear it and continued on up to the barricade to see for herself. She leapt up onto the make shift rampart to immediately see two Mechs being cut down by crossfire. The creatures were only able to get through in small numbers and were little trouble for the commandos, and yet they kept coming.

"Crazy bastards keep running onto our guns!" called one of the troops next to her.

She thought back to the lives Jafar and Tsengal had described. It was a hard and bitter existence for their race. She wondered if the first wave were just testing the defences, or even just expending their opponent's ammunition. She didn't share her thoughts. She wanted them to enjoy any little victory they could. The Colonel turned and jumped back down, striding to Warren's position.

"Keep it up, Major."

She strolled on more confidently than she had arrived. They had all expected to be hit with overwhelming force, and yet they were holding steady. The more she thought about it, the more it unsettled her until she decided to turn to Tsengal for answers.

"Why do they attack in such small number? This is too easy."

"This is just the beginning," he replied.

"Why not amass their forces for an assault?"

"My former leaders would not care for lives lost. The order to attack would have been given and must be followed."

"And you lived like that?"

"Until we met Major Taylor, there was no other way to live."

They got to the end of Warren's troops to find a seamless transition to Chen's soldiers. She was glad to see there was no break in the line. As she arrived, the guns went silent. She could see the first wave was finished. The Chinese troops had just four wounded and stood triumphantly before several dozen of the enemy. The soldiers were taking the hiatus to reload and ready themselves for a second wave. Chandra was about to congratulate Chen when they heard a ruckus from over the defences.

"Drones!" she heard one cry.

A surge of gunfire opened up, and she jumped to the

line to see for herself. The hover drones they had gotten used to seeing in France were pouring in like ants. Their weapons fired the second they came into view, and there seemed no end to their number. She lifted her rifle and quickly joined in the fight.

Gunfire poured in from above their heads, and she looked up to see several platoons of Chen's troops on a platform above them. Tsengal and four of her platoon leapt up to join in the fight, but they were all that could fit in the space left. Pulses from the drones smashed into their positions, but much of the defensive line was made from alien metal and stopped the worst of it.

The drones were being smashed as quickly as they poured into the hall, but still they kept coming. Several of the troops fired grenades into the mass, sending debris sprawling out across the ground and pelting the walls. Chandra's magazine ran dry, so she ducked back down behind the cover to load in a fresh one. Back on her feet, she could see the drones had made a couple of metres progress, despite the floor being littered with the wreckage of those that came before them. Pulses continued to smash their position and rush overhead. Clearly, the fire from the humans overwhelmed them.

Seeing the relentless push of the drones was a frightful sight. Even the aliens themselves could eventually be broken and forced into retreat, but the drones kept going until the bitter end. She remembered studying the use of them in human history, and how they fell out of favour due to the inhuman nature of them. Hearts and minds is what she always remembered.

The last of the drones were finally reduced to a line of twisted and burnt metal, and the hall was silent again. There were no cries of celebration. Destroying machines seemed to have little effect on their morale, but it was at least a relief to have stopped the first attack.

* * *

Taylor sat silently as the information from Red 1 was relayed to them on the briefing table. The bridge was quiet as they listened to the audio relay from Bradley until the moment contact was lost. For ten whole seconds after the feed went dead, no one said a word. Taylor looked up to the Admiral and pleaded.

"We have to go to their aid. We have to do something!"

Huber shook his head.

"We can't just leave them there and sit on our asses!"

Huber liked the Major, but he didn't like anyone raising his voice on his bridge, and telling him what he should and shouldn't do.

"You will do exactly as is ordered and expected of you. You heard your Colonel. They have ample ability and strength to hold the colony."

Taylor fell silent. He knew he could not challenge the

Admiral's decision. Huber turned to his XO.

"Double the range our scouts are going. I want to know if anything is heading our way."

He turned back to Taylor and could see the sadness in his face.

"Follow me, Major."

The two of them stepped inside the Admiral's quarters where they could talk freely. Taylor remained silent. He expected a grilling for his performance, but it didn't come.

"Please do not think I want to leave them out there, but remember this war is about more than one officer, more than one battalion, more than one army. This fleet is the only thing standing between the enemy and Earth. Would you risk it all far into enemy territory, when we still know so little? We created this fleet to protect Earth and our other colonies. When we can be certain that we have the ability and strength to move forward, we shall. But don't let yourself believe that one victory means we are all powerful."

Taylor accepted his words. He knew the Admiral was right, but it was a harsh reality to accept.

"I thought we were coming here to take the fight to the enemy, Sir."

"And we have, but now we must consolidate and defend what we have taken. This is a major breakthrough for our civilisation. We have travelled light years from Earth, invaded alien territory, and seized one of their colonies.

Let's not forget how far we have gotten. It was not so long ago that Earth was on its knees."

"Yes, Sir."

"Go now, calm yourself, and remember your Colonel is more than capable of taking care of herself."

Taylor showed himself out and skulked miserably off the bridge. By the time he had reached the elevator, his sadness was gone, and it was replaced by anger and a pig-headed resolve. When the doors opened, he strode out with purpose. He rushed towards the berths where Inter-Allied were living. Silva was the first familiar face he found.

"Sergeant, gather the troops. We're heading out."

The Sergeant looked puzzled.

"Sir, aren't we…"

"You heard me, Sergeant!"

Silva was never one to disobey his orders and quickly turned, rushing off to carry them out. Taylor lifted up his comms unit.

"Captain Ryan, prepare the Deveron for take-off."

"Roger that," came the reply.

He turned quickly to rush to his quarters to get his gear when he found himself confronted by Parker. She blocked his way and brought him to an abrupt halt. He could see from the look on her face that she had been listening in and did not approve.

"Don't do it."

"Don't do what? Help our friends?"

"Don't throw your life away again. Last time you were left to rot in prison because you disobeyed an order, and as a result a friend died, anyway. The Colonel is more than capable of looking after herself. The best thing you can do for her is to do as she asked, and protect the fleet."

He wanted to disagree and knew he could quite easily ignore everything she said, but deep down she was right.

"Why do we have to leave so many friends behind?" he asked.

"Why do we have to fight this damn war in the first place? I know she means a lot to you, but she does to all of us. You know what she'd want you to do."

He shook his head in disbelief.

"How can we just leave them there?"

"She may just surprise you yet. The Colonel is a hell of a woman."

"Yeah, she is."

"So what's it gonna be?"

Taylor thought for a few seconds, and she could already see he'd come to accept the grim turn of events. He lifted up his comms unit once again.

"Captain Ryan, belay that order. Sergeant Silva, stand down."

He looked back to Eli and was thankful she'd been there to stop him, but still in his heart, he knew it was the wrong thing to do. Eli lifted her hand and rested her palm on his cheek. She didn't envy his position as second in command.

"I am sick of this fucking war," he whispered.

"I know," she replied even more quietly as she leant into his shoulder.

"It'll be the death of us all."

"Don't talk like that. We've made it this far. What makes you think we can't see this through?"

"Just how much more luck do you think we have? We're put on the frontline every time. We can't go on like this forever."

"Well then I guess we better just win this war soon."

He smiled in response. A little light humour was the only thing that would break him from the cycle.

* * *

Chandra leapt down from Chen's position and rushed on to find Klimenko. In a war where they had little communications or visual displays, she had to see it all for herself. She could hear Suarez cursing under his breath at having to follow her, but she didn't care.

As she reached the Russian lines, she could see a number of dead who had been set aside and several wounded being carried away. The battle was clearly already over. Along the defensive wall, the marines had propped up Reitech shields in a regimented fashion every metre, providing protection and firing positions that resembled the ramparts of an old castle.

Major Klimenko sat at a table with a box of ammunition on the ground beside him, reloading his magazines. Several of his marines were with him. He looked surprisingly calm as his troops helped the wounded and adjusted the defences around him. As she approached, he peered up and greeted her.

"A good start, Colonel."

She leapt up onto the line of defences to peer over at the destruction below. The bodies of several dozen Mechs lay there. Some of the marines were passing through the enemy wounded, and she watched as one of the Russians fired two shots into one of the aliens that was still struggling.

Nothing seemed to shock her any longer, and she could see the rest of the troops had become just as polarised. She turned and jumped back down to address Klimenko.

"Any news on their strength?" he asked.

"Sorry, all I can say for sure is it's big."

He nodded in acceptance. "Any possibility of reinforcement?"

"Not likely. I'd think plenty of the enemy fleet have continued on to the gate."

"Do we present enough of a threat to draw some of their attentions and give Huber a fighting chance?"

"Hell, yes. I'm sure they're already well aware they'll need more than a few hundred soldiers to take this colony back. We'll make them pay a high price here."

"And ourselves? What price will we pay?"

"Whatever we have to. Our fate is now tied to this planet. Nobody leaves."

"I wasn't intended on going anywhere," he replied dryly.

"We're in this for the long haul. I'll arrange further supplies to be brought to you, presently."

He nodded, and she turned to return to where she had come from. The CP was still as silent as when she had left. The five personnel inside all turned to her for news. She was hoping for answers from them, but they had little information to share.

"The first wave has been held off. Casualties are as minimal as could be hoped for."

There was a small sigh of relief that was barely audible from several inside.

"Have you got any news on their numbers and the state of their fleet?" she continued.

"We still have a few camera feeds open. About half of the enemy ships continued on for the jump gate. The others have remained in orbit over our position."

"Then they must be readying themselves for a proper assault. They tested our defences today. I would not be surprised if the next wave comes before the day is over."

No one responded. They didn't want to speculate at what horrors they might face next.

"Have we got any means of contacting the fleet at all?"

she asked.

"The only possibility is to send a physical message aboard a ship or something similar, like one of the delivery drones."

*Delivery drones. It's time we put drones back into action,* she thought.

"Do you believe such a message would get through?"

Bradley shrugged his shoulders.

"We have no idea what's out there now, or what capabilities they have for stopping whatever we send out."

"That's reassuring."

"Sorry, Colonel."

"It's alright, there's nothing worth saying yet, anyhow."

She turned, leaving the room in silence once again. Tsengal was the first thing she saw as she stepped outside.

"They will not stop," he stated.

"We will break their armies over this colony."

"I have no doubt, but they will never give it up."

"Then let's make them pay a bitter price for it."

She carried on to Warren's position, as it was where she felt most at home. Chandra didn't like having to fight a battle without the 2nd Inter-Allied soldiers she had become so close to. Several wounded were being carted through to designated rooms with sealable environments. The breaches in the colony walls were causing oxygen shortages through much of the complex.

Chandra reached the commandos' position and

stepped up again to their defensive line. Dozens of the marines were busy rebuilding and improving the walls. Many others waited with their rifles at the ready for the next assault. Major Warren paced up to talk her privately.

"Do you think the General will send any help?"

"It'll be sometime before he could organise and get troops here. I fear they will be a long time short of reaching us in our time of need."

"So we're fucked. Left out here alone?"

"Pretty much. But we have a chance to make a difference. We have the opportunity to make those bastards pay a dear price."

She looked out to the carnage. There had been no attempt to clear the enemy dead. They provided obstacles to the next assault, if nothing else. Despite wearing a fully enclosed suit with her own oxygen supply, she could smell the burning bodies and armour. The taste and putrid smell was something she could never forget, and despite her suit protecting her from it, her mind projected it for her.

"They'll come in much greater number next time. Make sure you keep plenty of ammunition handy. If we can keep them bottlenecked in these hallways, we have a chance."

"A chance for what?" asked Warren.

"For victory."

He appeared surprised and looked into eyes to see if she truly meant it. He could tell she believed her own words. He just wasn't sure what she defined as victory.

"We'll nail those bastards. This planet will run in blue rivers of blood."

# CHAPTER NINE

Looking out to space, Taylor could see nothing but their own fleet and the deep abyss beyond. He waited to see an enemy ship every moment and fully expected it, but nothing came. He sat on a viewing deck close to the outer skin of the Washington's hull with a real view out to space. It always felt different seeing it with one's own eyes than on a projected display. The window was just a metre wide and had a large blast door slung over it, ready to shut at a moment's notice.

Where Mitch stood was one of the few luxuries of the ship. It was quiet and relaxing, and the view out to space made it feel so much less claustrophobic than the rest of the vessel. He imagined the feeling was much like that of working aboard a submarine in their oceans; a job he never envied. Living at sea was something he always enjoyed, but the notion of the environment outside being fatal made

Taylor feel sick at times.

A hand reached onto his shoulder and even though he wore his armour, he could feel it was a light touch. It could only be one person in the world. He felt his shoulders relax from the highly-strung state he had been in and turned with a smile to see Eli.

"You need some rest," she whispered.

"Don't we all?"

Her weary face tightened into an even broader smile.

*How can she remain so positive?* He wondered.

"I'll sleep when I'm in the grave," Taylor added.

Her smile quickly vanished, and she responded quickly.

"Many men have said the same, and it has come sooner than they would have liked. Don't think just because you have made it this far, you are invincible. You can be killed just the same as us all."

"No, not me."

She shook her head, but she could not quite tell if he was joking or not.

"Please get some sleep," she pleaded.

"Will you join me?" he asked with a smirk.

"No chance, rest is the only thing you're good for."

He knew she was right, and there was nothing more to be said about it. He slipped away from her hand and carried on to his quarters without another word. By the time he had reached his door, he knew just how exhausted he was, and it was a wonder he was still on his feet.

Seconds after stripping his exo suit off, Mitch had collapsed onto his bed with his boots still on. He fell into a deep sleep that was void of all the horrors he had fretted over the past days. Before he knew it, a buzzer was ringing beside him with a call coming through. He looked to his watch, and it showed three hours had passed. The last thing he remembered was propping his rifle in the corner of his quarters. He coughed to clear his throat and sat up in a daze. Despite that, he already felt ten times better than before his rest. He smashed his hand down on the comms channel.

"Taylor," he said in a croaky voice.

"Sir, your presence is requested on the bridge, immediately."

"Roger that."

He stood up and quickly stretched out to feel his body was remarkably rested after the few short but good hours of sleep he had gotten. He'd have killed for a shower, but more urgent matters were at hand. Within a few minutes, he was out the door and making a quick dash to the bridge. The doors opened, and it was clear Huber had been waiting for him.

"News from Red 1, Major."

He rushed to the side of the table in hope of some good word of Chandra's progress.

"The Colonel continued to transmit data until their signal was jammed."

"Are they holding out?" he asked briskly.

"Certainly up till that point, yes. It seems much of the enemy fleet passed them by and are heading for us. This means we cannot risk sending any support to the planet."

"Nothing? We're just going to leave them there?"

"They're going to have to slug it out, as are we. Now, I suggest you look to our own situation."

Taylor quickly understood there was much more to the story than Huber had passed on.

"You have received confirmed reports they are heading this way?"

The Admiral nodded and sighed deeply.

"They're coming for us with, well, maybe not everything they have, but a lot. We have gotten this far by taking the enemy by surprise, but now we will see what it is truly like to face an organised enemy."

"Sorry, Sir, but I have already seen it enough times, and it ain't pretty."

"Mmm," mumbled the Admiral.

"How long do we have?"

"Hard to say exactly, but best estimate is about five hours."

"What are your intentions?"

"We will hold this position while it is still possible."

"And if it becomes impossible?"

The Admiral looked up into Taylor's eyes and could see he had already accepted they might have to leave people behind. Taylor shook his head in disgust. He knew they should have sent support to Chandra, and he knew they could have done so when he asked for it, but it was all too late now.

"It will be a bloody day."

"That much is certain. Have your marines ready to defend this ship. I do not want a repeat of our last action. We came very nearly close to losing the Washington, and that is not acceptable."

"Several thousand tonnes of metal lost is not, but several thousand lives are."

Taylor did not ask it as a question and did not expect any kind of response. Huber hated the situation as much as he did, but neither blamed each other for either turn of events. Mitch turned and left the bridge. He knew there was nothing more to discuss. There was no more news to come, only the swarm of the enemy. He lifted up his communicator.

"Inter-Allied, those not on watch have one hour of rest, after which everyone is on active duty until ordered otherwise. All officers to assemble in thirty minutes at briefing room B."

On open channels, he knew all would know the enemy were close and bearing down on them, but he couldn't hide it from them any longer. He swung by the canteen on the way to the meet in the hope of filling his hunger. All he got was some artificial piece of junk that supposedly contained real meat, but you wouldn't know it.

Fifteen minutes after he put out the call, he sat in the room awaiting the others and finished the God-awful food he'd been given. Despite its dire taste and texture, he felt remarkably better after finishing it. Jones was the first to join him, early as usual.

"I assume by your lack of urgency that we are not flying out in support of the Colonel?" he asked.

The words had left his mouth before he'd even taken a seat. It rubbed salt into the wound that one of his best friends was so bitterly disappointed.

"That is not a decision for us to make."

"And yet you tried to."

Taylor looked into his eyes and could see a smile appear on the Captain's face.

"Your continuing lack of regard for authority is truly astonishing. It is a miracle you have gotten this far. Any other man would have been kicked out a long time ago."

Taylor laughed. It was not so much Jones' thoughts that amused him, but the fact he didn't pull any punches on making it clear.

"I cannot fight every battle in this war," replied Taylor.

"No, and you'd do well to remember it."

It was not long before the rest of his officers had gathered. They were all competent and reliable companions, but Taylor could not help feel saddened by how few had been with him since the start. It was a bitter reminder of how mortal he was. They all sat silently, awaiting his words. He was in charge of the entire Battalion for this battle and the defence of the flagship, and it weighed heavily on his mind.

"An enemy fleet descends upon us. We've got just a few hours until all hell breaks loose. We don't know how many they are, but it is a substantial force. You should know this. The Washington is the most important ship of the fleet. Its loss would have a detrimental effect on our activities in this system. I fully intend to go to the support of Red 1 and our troops there once this is over. Let's keep this ship in one piece, and ensure we leave no one behind."

"Detrimental effect, Major?" asked Jackson.

Taylor sighed. He didn't want to imagine the situation.

"If we lose the Washington, it is my belief that this task force would consider any further presence here to endanger the remainder of the fleet, and would therefore carry out an immediate withdrawal through the gateway."

"What about the troops on Red 1?" Grey asked.

The room went silent. They all realised what Taylor was saying, but none wanted to believe it could happen.

"The best thing we can do for the Colonel, and those with her, is to give all that we have here. We need a decisive victory."

The facts of their situation made Taylor feel sick to his stomach. Having to voice his thoughts only made it worse.

"The enemy will be with us within a few hours,

maybe less. You all know your jobs. You have all been allocated your areas. Remember, that as soon as we lose our communications, all can go to hell. Keep in contact at all times. Ensure that both I and the Admiral know your status and enemy movements at all times."

"And if the Washington was to fall?" asked Ota.

Taylor sighed heavily.

"Pray that it doesn't. Anymore questions?"

"Are the crew armed and ready this time to assist in the defence of the ship?" asked Jones.

"All personnel who are able have been issued weapons and placed at the defence of key strategic points. They are certainly armed, but ready? Remember when you first faced this enemy on the beaches of France. Imagine that fight where there was nowhere left to run, that is where they're at."

"Where will you be through this engagement?"

"For now, I'll be heading to the bridge to monitor the situation with the Admiral. I'll want one platoon posted to me at all times, and Jafar will be with me also. I'll be playing it by ear and going where and when I am needed. Anything else?"

They shook their heads.

"All of you, we've fought some tough fights through this war and made it through. I don't want to end it all up here in the blackness of space. If I am going to die, may it be on solid ground and on my own land. Let's give these bastards a good kicking, and remind them why they don't mess with the human race."

Several of the officers smiled at the sentiment, but the stress of the situation had them refrain from being overly excited. They all feared what was coming for them. Not knowing the enemy strength was the worst of all. Taylor sat still as the others left the room, except for Jones. After the door finally shut behind them, he spoke.

"I don't care what happens in this battle, but promise me you will not let me be taken alive?"

Taylor smiled.

"You aren't going anywhere. You have a wife and girlfriend to return for."

Jones stared at him.

"After everything I have seen, I'll enjoy every free moment I have left in this world."

"I was being serious. You're gonna make it through this, same as me. We've survived all this time. We can't die now."

"We can all die," replied Jones.

Taylor stood up and placed his hand on the Captain's shoulder.

"That is not the Jones I have come to know. We're gonna give these bastards hell and live to celebrate with a few beers."

"I bloody well hope so, and Colonel Chandra better be there beside us!"

He got up and strolled out of the room. They both knew it would not be that easy, and Taylor was not under any illusion that it could be the last battle for all of them. Taylor left the room to find Jafar patiently waiting for him.

"What are you doing here?"

"The enemy is close now. I will remain by your side until this is over."

"We're going to win, you know."

"I had no doubt of that, but I should like to remain at your side throughout."

"You will not be allowed on the bridge during this fight. Plenty have come to trust you, but it does not extend that far."

"Then I shall remain outside the door when you are inside."

"Well, alright then."

Taylor made his way back to the bridge. The corridors were quiet now. He passed several gun emplacements with Navy personnel standing at the ready. There was nothing left to do. Positions had been taken, and ammunition had been issued. They waited for those bearing down on them.

The bridge was equally quiet as Taylor entered. He was glad to see the entrance had been strengthened and reinforced with a number of guards. The Admiral sat back in his chair, watching the scanners as if in a daydream.

"Sir, we're ready for 'em," Taylor said.

Huber casually turned his head and nodded, remaining

in the dreamy state.

"All the technology in the world, and yet we are still so often in the dark. Intelligence, reconnaissance, communication, these are out weaknesses now."

"Yes, it is difficult to live once again in a communication dark age," he replied.

"Not knowing is the worst thing in the world. We could have a fleet large enough to end the war, or we could be awaiting our destruction."

The Admiral was speculating in a quiet voice that only Taylor could hear, as they were so close to each other. Before he could answer, a siren went off, and they quickly turned to see several objects on the scanners.

"Sir, we've got confirmed enemy incoming!" shouted Vega.

The Admiral sprung to life and jumped onto his feet.

"How many?"

Vega went silent as he carefully studied the screens.

"Twelve targets so far, with more incoming. At their present speed, they will be in range within five minutes."

"Launch the rest of our fighters and prepare to fire!"

The last of the craft on the Washington scrambled. The crews had been waiting for the call, and all were streaming out of the docking bays within two minutes. There was some relief on the bridge that the waiting game was over, but now a new dread overshadowed them.

Huber tapped a few buttons and brought up a zoomed

display of what was coming at them. Several of the bridge crew gasped when they saw the horde of ships. Many of the Naval personnel had only ever seen one action, and that was a surprise attack on the enemy at the gateway. A determined and organised attack by the Krycenaeans was never something any of them could get used to.

"In range of our primary weapons in sixty seconds."

"Fire when you have a solution," replied Huber.

Taylor stood silently and prayed they had enough power to hold off the enemy. It was not himself he thought of, but Chandra and the others they had left behind. He wondered in every free moment he had how she was doing. He knew she'd be knee deep in enemy bodies, and that at least brought him some relief.

"We have a firing solution, weapons hot, fire when ready!" Vega shouted over the intercom.

The Washington's big guns opened fire first and were soon joined by the other carrier and the larger vessels in the fleet. The space around them was lit up like a fireworks display as railgun rounds soared towards the incoming enemy. Two of the enemy ships, which appeared to be frigate in size, were completely obliterated in the initial salvo.

The hulks of the wrecked ships continued on, but most of their outer structures were blasted out and smashed into several other enemy ships. The incoming craft opened fire seconds after being struck. The Washington was screened by dozens of ships in the human fleet, meaning it saw little of the opening volley.

Pulses smashed into the frigates and destroyers around them, but most continued to lay down fire against the enemy. Taylor had never had the luxury of watching such a battle from afar, and it struck him how relentless the enemy were in the pursuit of human destruction. Never was there any attempt at communication or any form of negotiation.

*Do they really want us all dead that badly?* He asked himself.

The enemy craft continued to rush towards them, despite their losses.

"We'll surely lose much of our communication as they come into range. It matters little, every man and woman in the fleet knows what they must do," Huber said to the crew of the bridge.

The enemy ships were still closing the distance at a rapid speed, and Taylor could see the human fighters closing in to engage.

"Their priority is to prevent any and all potential boarding actions," Huber whispered to Taylor.

"They put me out of a job then," he replied dryly.

Huber shook his head in astonishment that the Major could be so calm and witty under pressure. It was a character trait he truly appreciated.

"Major, I'm not sure even the President of the United States could put you out of a job."

"No," he muttered as he looked out to the enemy ships, "but they might."

The overlay screen that gave them a three hundred and sixty degree view cut out, and the report of the loss of communications soon came in. They were left with a few fixed video feeds and hard lines to comms around their own ship only. By all accounts, they were in the dark yet again.

Taylor and Huber stood beside each other and watched as half a dozen of their ships advanced past the Washington to provide a further buffer to the Capitol ship. Their previous engagements had taught them all a lot about the weaknesses in their defences.

One of the displays lit up with a bright burst as one of the human frigates was struck and burst into six pieces. The immense loss of life weighed heavily on both their hearts, but they could now do nothing but watch. In that moment, Taylor got a taste of the sense of emotion their leaders must go through. They had to stand and watch as men and women were killed, pursuing their directives. It left Mitch feeling hollow and disgusted. There was rarely a time he wished to face the enemy in person, but this was one of the occasions, if only to save him from the sickening display before them.

The Washington's guns continued to roar with a continuous barrage. Through the hail of gunfire and pulses, they could begin to see the extent of the enemy fleet. It was sizeable, but by no means overwhelming. The combined human fleets had obliterated the first wave of enemy ships, and it had a great impact on their strength.

One of the enemy hulks floated quickly towards the Anglesey, one of their destroyers. Evasive manoeuvres were not quick enough, and the hulk smashed into the tail section of the destroyer. The impact ripped a great tear in the outer hull of the ship, and they could see a dozen bodies rush out from the breach.

The Anglesey was smashed off course but remained intact. Its forward guns continued to fire as other crews rushed to secure the breach and put out the fires.

*They're going to make it*, Huber smiled in relief, but it was in vain. Six huge pulses smashed into the destroyer's hull and ripped it in two.

"My God," whispered Huber.

The bridge crew were utterly silent as they watched the devastation unfolding. They could do nothing now but rely on the gun crews and pilots to do their jobs. They watched for another five minutes as the enemy fleet came to a halt, and the fleets duked it out like old ships of the line.

Friendly fighters ducked and weaved in between the battle, preying on the alien transports as they tried to breach the lines of frigates and reach the carriers. As they watched, two such transports burst into fragments, another three punched through a hole in the perimeter.

"Sir, they are on intercept course with us," said Vega hastily.

"Bring the bastards down!" Huber screamed.

They watched a wing of three human fighters bank hard and engage the three ships. They got out an initial burst of fire but were cut down from cannons from the enemy vessels. Two of the fighters exploded immediately, and the other was blown off course.

"Target our guns on those ships!" ordered Huber.

Vega was already relaying the commands before the Admiral had even finished giving them. Taylor watched with bated breath as the ships rushed towards them. He felt his hands grip tighter around the briefing table. As much as he didn't want to see the Washington be compromised, he was desperate to get stuck in with the fight rather than watch it from afar.

"Destroy them!" Huber shouted.

The Washington's guns opened fire with a vicious burst, destroying one of the enemy transports in its first volley. The second damaged one of the others, but they had passed within the range of many of the guns. The Kittyhawk rushed to their aid and fired rapidly at the leading enemy craft, and with one concentrated burst, smashed it off course, causing its hull to twist into a burning wreck.

They all watched the remaining enemy ship that was already damaged, still hurtle towards them. It was larger than the transports they had faced at the gateway, and Taylor was already trying to estimate the number of Mechs it might carry. A couple of hundred was his best guess, but he prayed he was wrong.

"We must have something left? Shoot the bastards down!" ordered Huber.

"Sir, they have passed within range of our guns. There's nothing more I can do."

"God damn it! Taylor, have your marines ready to repel the breach!"

Mitch was about to leap into action when he caught a sign of movement out of the corner of his eye. He looked closer to the display screen.

"Admiral, look!"

Huber rushed to his side and looked down to see two of the Washington's fighters swoop in on a sharp arc towards the transport, running its length and strafing as they went. The bursts of gunfire ripped into the hull, but it kept moving. As the fighters passed, they spun around and continued to pour fire into the transport, continuing at the same speeds backwards. At the last moment, they put their engines on full as they approached the carrier.

The enemy transport was a complete wreck, but it still smashed into the hull at a fair speed. At the bridge, they couldn't feel the impact against the vast carrier, but they could see the hole it smashed into the lower decks. After tearing a huge gouge in the Washington, the ruined transport merely floated past. Huber sighed in relief.

"Have those decks sealed off and repair crews sent immediately! Taylor get some of your troops down there to protect the crews whilst they work."

He looked back to the frontline and could see the enemy attack had been smashed over the defensive wall of the fleet. Many of the ships continued to fire out at the remaining enemy ships, but he could see that most had already begun to flee.

"Do we pursue them?" asked Vega.

"No, continue to lay down fire while they are in range, and redress our formation as our communications come back on line."

"Sir, this may be our only chance to finish them."

"Count ourselves lucky, Captain. We fought the enemy on their terms in their system, and we won. Let's not get ahead of ourselves. Wouldn't you agree, Major?"

Taylor didn't like being put on the spot in opposition to the XO, but he certainly did agree with the Admiral from a tactical perspective.

"Yes, Sir, we should take the time to repair and restore what we have, and get to the aid of our forces on Red 1."

Huber smiled at Mitch's well-timed retort.

"Sir, communications are back online."

"Do we have contact with the rest of the fleet?"

"Yes, Sir."

"Open up a channel."

Huber took a deep breath, and after the nod from his XO, he began.

"This is Admiral Huber. I want to congratulate you all on a job well done, but before I go any further, let me ask you all to organise any assistance you can to our comrades. We have crippled ships, stranded personnel. Let's look to our own."

He waited briefly to see that Vega had already begun working to the order, and knew he could carry on with it already underway.

"We won a valuable victory here today. The enemy knew we were here, and that is what they sent to fight us. They underestimated you all. They underestimated your courage, your strength, and your fortitude. Thank you all. May we remember those who fell today, for as long as we live. Congratulations to you all. Huber out."

He sighed deeply and sat down. Taylor could see the Admiral was utterly exhausted. The whole situation weighed heavily on their minds, and Taylor's mind and body felt as if he'd been out there fighting them with his own hands.

"I don't envy you," Taylor said quietly.

"Nor I you," he replied.

"Then we must be in the right jobs."

Taylor laughed. He could tell his suggestion of supporting Red 1 passed the Admiral by. It was not that he was not listening, but that Huber was a rightfully cautious man. Taylor already knew he could do little to change his mind, but that would not stop him trying.

"Sir, may I have permission to attempt to break the siege of Red 1 and bring our people back?"

"I am sorry, Major, but you know our situation here. With the several thousand troops we have, we have too few to protect the ships of this fleet. It is not just this carrier that is in danger of boarding by the enemy. The enemy attack was repulsed, but not without cost. You can guarantee they will return in far greater number. You know this enemy. They will not quit because of their losses. They do not care for their losses. They will keep coming at us until they finish the job."

"And so we just stay here and get slowly whittled away until there is nothing left?"

"General White has gone for reinforcements. The shipyards of Earth and the colonies are putting out new ships on a daily basis. Crews are prepared at the same speed, and ground troops are in plenty of supply to fill any transports sent this way. We will hold this location until they arrive. If we reach a position where we are confident of our defence here, then I will let you go to your Colonel's aid."

"And when will that be, when they are all dead and buried?"

"I am sorry, Major, but we cannot endanger the lives of all in this fleet for the few. Red 1 is a defensible position.

If anyone can hold there, it is Colonel Chandra."

"She is an incredible officer, Sir, but she is not a miracle worker. Their ammunition will not last forever, nor will their food. They are under siege."

Taylor's voice faded off. He knew it was useless to go on any further. He had already accepted the Admiral's decision before he'd even started, but he had to try.

"Have your marines revert to watches and those not on duty get as much rest as they can. We all need to remain clearheaded and ready to do our jobs to the best of our abilities."

The Admiral's commanding voice echoed through his ears, and he quickly stood up and saluted, turning to go about his duties. He stepped out of the bridge to find Jafar and Parker awaiting him with her platoon.

"What are you doing here?" he asked her.

"You requested a platoon at your service."

"And that just happened to be yours?" he asked with a smile.

"Is it true that we whopped 'em?" she asked.

"Oh yes, well and truly, but they still came close to boarding the Washington. One of the destroyers was boarded during the fight but managed to hold out."

"Of course, they did. Marines do their jobs."

Sergeant Silva rushed around the corner to address Taylor.

"Sir, what are your orders?"

"Have the Company stand down. I want double strength watches of all districts."

"The fight is really over, Sir?" he asked in surprise.

"We aren't the only ones who are fighting this war, Sergeant. The Navy boys did some fine work today. We can rest for another day."

"Some of us can."

Taylor knew he was referring to those left on Red 1, but he didn't have the heart to explain the situation. All he now thought about were those left behind, and all he wanted to do was go to their aid.

# CHAPTER TEN

Earth was a beautiful sight, which was a little different to human eyes after seeing the barren alien world and Mars. General White stood at the front of the bridge as they descended on his homeworld. He wondered every minute of every day how Admiral Huber was getting along. He was confident that with Taylor at his side things would work out.

"Landing in thirty minutes, Sir."

"Thank you," he replied.

The Earth defence grid they passed was an impressive sight. It had been little more than foundations when they departed for Tau Ceti. Three-dozen warships occupied the space above Earth, and more were joining them all the time. White could see that Earth was ready for the enemy. He just hoped they were ready to help those he left behind in alien lands.

The thirty minutes passed quickly. After days of waiting for this moment, the General was eager to make his point. As the representative of the fleet and Earth's first ever journey into foreign systems, a large party had formed to greet him. Countries' leaders and Generals lined the landing zone at his base, in eager anticipation of some news.

As the ramp of his ship lowered to the ground, he realised he was being greeted by not only the President of the United States, but Presidents, Prime Ministers and Kings of a dozen or more countries. He sighed deeply.

"We're in for a long day."

\* \* \*

"Incoming!"

Chandra's feet had been propped up on an ammunition crate, and she had almost gotten a few minutes' sleep when she was awoken. Her survival instinct kicked in, and she leapt to her feet. A second later, gunfire opened up from friendly forces nearby. Suarez rushed up to her with his rifle at the ready.

"They got the drop on us, and they're trying to sneak in!"

"What?"

She was in shock. It wasn't the sort of tactics she had ever seen or heard of being used by the enemy.

"Our scouts caught sight of them a minute ago!"

She lifted her rifle and rushed to the defensive wall. She'd stationed herself besides Warren and his commandos. The Major was already on top of the wall, taking carefully aimed shots.

"Give me an update!" she yelled.

"A few dozen lightly equipped hostiles breached the perimeter, nothing we have seen before. They're agile, fast and sneaky."

Tsengal jumped up beside them and had just heard the last few words.

"They're cave people, primitive in their lifestyle but good hunters and faster than most. They lack much of the strength of my people, but they are well suited to many tasks."

"Closest thing to scouts we have seen yet. That's what we'll call the bastards," replied Chandra. "Have you killed any?"

Warren nodded.

"A few, but the rest of the sneaky bastards have taken cover amongst the rubble and bodies. We can advance and try to flush them out."

Chandra looked to Tsengal for advice.

"I would not recommend it. They will lure you into traps and divide your number. The best defence against them is to stay strong in number behind these defences."

"Alright. Warren, have this information and my orders

passed down the line. I want sharpshooters present and active at all times. Maybe we can't hunt them down, but we can sure knock a few heads off when they're good enough to present them."

'Yes, Ma'am."

Several shots rang out behind their position and she turned quickly to see one of the new enemies darting back behind cover. The shots skimmed the armour of a fallen creature, but the new one went unharmed.

"Hold your fire!"

The troops turned in surprise at their Colonel's command.

"They're baiting us. Trying our defences, expending ammunition. I want allocated sharp shooters only. The rest of you are to keep your eyes open and spot for future attacks! Pass the word!"

"Can I have a word?" Warren asked.

She nodded in agreement and gestured for him to follow her to a quiet spot around a corner towards the CP.

"What is it?" she asked hastily.

Warren could tell she was highly strung, but he could not wait any longer.

"They aren't coming for us, are they? Not the fleet, not the General, not Major Taylor, we're on our own, aren't we?"

Chandra took in a deep breath and looked away. She didn't want to answer that. She didn't want to have to tell him, nor admit their situation to herself. They were deep in the shit, and there seemed little to be done about it but fight for every minute of life they could.

"Maybe, maybe they'll come, maybe we're on our own. I just don't know anymore."

Her voice became shaky, and Warren could see she was close to tears, but they would never come, no matter how bad things got. She was too strong and too dignified to ever be seen crying, as much as her heart might want it.

"So yes, this might be the end for us. We may never leave this shithole planet ever again. How do you want to end, crawling on your hands and knees, or like a hero?" she asked.

He looked deep into her eyes and righted himself, realising she would not show an ounce of weakness. It was not in her. He stood twenty-five centimetres taller than the slight Colonel and substantially broader built. It made him feel a slither of shame that she never doubted them in their darkest hour.

"I'm not going anywhere, Colonel."

"No, none of us are by the looks of things."

"I'll stand by you no matter the outcome, as will every one of the men and women under my command."

"It was never in doubt. You've done sterling work under my command, just as I know you did through the first war. You were brought here for a reason, Major, because you're a damn fine officer commanding some of our very best."

\* \* \*

Huber stood in a daze again as he looked at the wrecks floating in the space around the gateway. Engineers and repair ships were working hard to patch up the ships that could be saved. Taylor could tell he was not used to seeing such carnage. He had not borne witness to the epic bloody land battles that had plagued much of the world in the first war.

"Do you think General White will be successful in convincing the powers that be to support us?"

Huber shook his head.

"I don't know anymore, Major. Maybe if they knew what had happened since he left the system. If they could know we have held this far. If they could see how bravely our people fought, then maybe."

"We should at least send a messenger through the gate and update them on our situation."

"We have strict orders not to use the gateway, except in need of complete withdrawal."

"Sir, those orders have been given by people who are not here. They don't know what we've seen, what we have faced. Information is key here. They need to know."

Taylor could see that Huber was losing faith in their endeavour. Depression was overpowering the great officer, and Mitch felt it was the restraints placed on the Admiral that were reducing him to such a state.

"Why would they send us out here if they weren't willing to support us?"

"Come with me."

He led Taylor through to his quarters. Mitch had gotten used to loathing going into the room, as he knew it likely meant bad news that had to be concealed from the rest of the crew. He poured out two glasses of whiskey and sat down with the sigh of a physically and mentally exhausted man. He slid one of the glasses over to Taylor.

"No thank you, Sir," Taylor said sternly.

"We live in such fearsome times. Humanity nearly reached its end before our very eyes, and now here we are, on the raggedy edge of a hostile system with our backs against the wall. I think a drink right now could go a long way to keeping a man from going mad."

Taylor looked down at the glass and could feel his lips wet at the sight of it. He'd remained stone cold sober since they came through to Tau Ceti, but maybe the Admiral was right. He picked up the glass and took a sip of the smooth scotch. Huber smiled and finally began to address his questions.

"The honest truth is that few world leaders supported this endeavour. A committee of Army, Navy and Marine and Air Force officers, such as myself and White, petitioned to the President to allow us to come here."

"Wow, you really pushed for this?"

"It may not be a pleasant experience, but it was the

right thing to do."

Taylor was starting to understand what that meant for them all. They didn't have even half the support he thought they would.

"Getting this fleet together was a massive undertaking, but we were not promised any additional troops. All of the senior officers in this fleet volunteered. They all knew the risks, and yet chose to follow me. General White is not so much going home to report our findings, but to plead for backup."

"My God, we pushed into enemy territory with no support. No supply network, no hope of reinforcement?"

"No hope? Look at how far we have come, from the near end of the world to faraway lands."

Taylor dipped his head into his left hand. Once again they were being pushed around like chess pieces, worth nothing more to the player than their moment in time.

"Do you believe White can get us the support we need?"

"I doubt it. None of the information he is taking back will make it anymore appealing to follow in our footsteps."

"Then what the hell are we doing here?"

Huber smashed his glass down on the table.

"What are we doing here? The same as we have always been doing. Our duty. Just because some idiots in office won't do what's right, that doesn't give the rest of us the excuse to bury our heads in the sand. This second war was coming whether we liked it or not. We're making sure this time we fight it on our own terms."

Taylor shook his head.

"I don't buy it. There's still more you aren't telling me. You are too practical a man to risk the entire fleet on such an endeavour."

"Yes. The honest truth is that enemy forces were already beginning to amass at the gateway in our system. You really think we had no intelligence on the area before we arrived there? Many of us could see what was coming. We were just weeks or months away from another invasion. The Earth defence grid and our fleets are well underway, but what hope could they have with the wolves at our door?"

Taylor breathed a sigh of relief. He didn't like being kept out of the loop, but he was glad to know there was a legitimate reason for their actions.

"Why on Earth could you not have told me this beforehand?"

"World leaders would not believe the information we put before them. We called their bluff. If the enemy truly were weak, then we could sail out and smash them in their own lands."

"That was just another manipulation."

"Yes, the only way to get the job done. We always knew this was a very dangerous mission. You were not lied to about that. We calculated that Earth needed three months to be prepared for a second invasion, and yet it appeared an enemy attack could take place with just four weeks."

Taylor sipped back on his drink.

*It's all becoming clear now.*

"So we are a buffer? Keep them away from our lands as long as possible?"

"That is one of our tasks, and to ensure they appreciate the severity of the situation. When the first war started, our military was ill prepared. They need to know what danger lies around the corner."

"And you believe we can make that difference?"

"We already have. I can't say how long we can hold here, but I can say we have already had an impact. Red 1 was clearly a key strategic point for the enemy, as is this gateway. We've inflicted substantial losses on them so far and continue to defend the entrance to our Solar System."

"Then send a messenger through the gateway. Let all on Earth know what we have done here, and that we still hold."

Huber went silent for a moment as he thought it over. They could both see it would serve to assist their purpose.

"Okay, we will send a single messenger within the hour, but I do not promise anything will come of it."

"Thank you, Sir."

Taylor thought about his next question carefully, as it was a delicate matter to put to their leader.

"Sir, you said, if the defence of this gateway becomes unrealistic, we will withdraw. Is that truly your intention?"

The Admiral looked offended for a second before he

could see how necessary the question was.

"Of course. I would never throw lives away needlessly. The time may well come when we have to return through that gate. We both still have people out there, friends and comrades. If the time comes, could you leave them behind to save what remains?"

Mitch knew the right answer to the question, but his heart made him want to say no.

"Sir, we could get them back. We could fire up this fleet, head for Red 1, and get our people back."

"Sure, we could try, but we both know the chances of us returning alive from such a mission would be minimal. The enemy forces have amassed at that planet. We have the strength to remain here in defence, but we do not have what we need to move forward."

Taylor knew the Admiral was right, but it didn't make it any easier.

* * *

General White had sat at a conference table for two hours discussing the events he had taken part in. He could see that several world leaders there were growing weary and seemed to be losing interest. It disgusted him that they would show as such, even if they did feel it. But he could not speak out against them. He needed the support of those around him. In his moment of need, Field Marshal

Copley spoke up. The proud British officer was a man White knew by reputation but had only met briefly.

"It seems clear to me that Admiral Huber's fleet is in need of assistance. They have made headway in their mission and in assisting them further, we secure the safety of our Solar System."

White nodded in gratitude for the support. Brigadier Dupont leapt to his feet in a typically dramatic nature they had come to expect of the Frenchman.

"I am sorry, but I am yet to see any progress other than provoking a race which since the war ended have shown no signs of further aggression."

White could feel his blood boil as he listened to the obnoxious man.

"Are you that naive that you believe the war to be over? You think they will simply give up and forget what happened here?"

"We are, General. We are moving on with our lives in peace."

White shook his head in astonishment.

"Asshole," he muttered under his breath.

"General White."

He turned to see the American President staring at him.

"Yes, Mr President."

"You are the only one among us who has been to this foreign system, Tau Ceti. You are therefore better informed and qualified than any one of us to recommend a way forward here. What do you believe we, as a united people, should do?"

"Sir, I have seen what this enemy is capable of. They will not stop. They will never stop. They will end us, or we will end them. Our fleets have made a great advance into enemy territory, and I believe with the backing of Earth's armies, we could remove this threat forever."

"Remove the threat?" asked President Moreau. "You are talking about genocide? Going to their homes and killing every man, woman and child in their race?"

"Yes, I am," replied White. "If we dealt with a civilised enemy, we could beat them into submission and end this war with some kind of peace. But we do not face a civilised enemy. They are a race of technologically advanced savages."

"And is that not what you are recommending that we become? We are taking on advances in our technology every day from what we have learnt from them, and now you want to become as bloodthirsty and murderous as they are?"

The General opened to his mouth to speak but stopped himself and panned around to study the faces of all around him. Most looked down on him as an upstart against the peace they now enjoyed. He laughed for a few seconds, so as not to cry.

"You now live the peaceful lives we all wanted, but do you not see that these perfect lives you now have are in danger yet again? Will you bury your heads in the sand and believe that we have once more seen an end to war? War will never be over, not whilst intelligent beings exist. We have a choice before us. We can sit back and await our destruction, or we can step up and fight for the peace you all so desperately want to secure."

The United States President sat at the centre and head of the discussion, and it was clear he played more than his equal part in the decision to be made. White had always liked the man. He had voted for him, after all. He could see President Walter wanted to support him, but he faced a vicious opposition.

"General, I think we all need an understanding of quite what you have in mind and the alternatives. As far as I understand it, you want to pursue a full scale campaign into Tau Ceti, and bring the enemy race to an end."

"Yes, Mr President. I believe the most apt analogy would be – 'If an injury has to be done to a man, it should be so severe that his vengeance need not be feared.'"

"I don't think reciting ancient philosophy is appropriate to our situation," snapped Dupont.

"Far from it, everything we know has been learnt from those who came before us. Would you cast aside their wisdom and re-invent the wheel?"

"Enough," said Walter sternly.

The President didn't need to shout. His deep and commanding voice was sufficient to resonate around the room and bring it to silence.

"You do not see another option?" he asked of White.

"Not if the future of the human race is to be persevered, Sir, no."

"And if, as the combined forces of Earth, we sent all our might to Tau Ceti to crush them, what would be the cost?"

"Probably hundreds of thousands of lives."

Gasps rang out across the room.

"You are surprised? Surprised that the cost of war is the lives of honourable and courageous men and women? The last war was not won by anyone else. I'd never send a marine to die unless I knew it had to be done. Would you prefer we lost enlisted men and women of our armies, navies and air force, or civilians? The price has to be paid somewhere. I believe we can end this for good, and save the people of this world from any future pain and suffering."

A cough rang out, and White looked to see Commander Kelly from the Moon Colony. He had been sitting quietly at the far end of the table throughout.

"Commander, I of course refer to humanity as a whole. I would see to the protection of the Moon equally with Earth."

Kelly nodded in appreciation. They all went silent for a solid minute as every one of them thought of the options before them. Finally, the US President spoke up, as he had led the meeting from the very start.

"It seems to me, General, that while in theory you might be right, we have too little information. We do not know the enemy strength. We do not know how many colonies they have. We do not know if we have the strength and resources to succeed in a war in faraway lands. As much as I think there is a chance you could be right, we cannot risk all with so little understanding of what lies ahead."

White looked around the room to see several were nodding in agreement. His argument was dead in the dirt, and he knew it. He thought about pleading further, but it was clearly going to be time wasted.

"I am sorry, General, but my advice would be to return to Admiral Huber. Congratulate him on a successful excursion into enemy territory, and have him return home with the brave men and women he commands. That is my recommendation and order to the forces of the United States. Are all in agreement?"

White's hopes had been dashed, and he got up with slumped shoulders. The taste of defeat was bitterer than ever when it came from his own people. The meeting was adjourned, and the officials scattered quickly. Just after he had left the room, Kelly stopped him for a word. White sighed. He had no more desire to talk.

"What can I do for you, Commander?"

"You're right. We both know it, but you must have known you'd never have convinced that room. They fought the last war because they had no choice."

"Maybe they don't have a choice now. They just don't see it yet."

"If that is the case, then they will rally to your cause soon enough."

"Taylor said you were a good man."

"Ha, what would he know?"

White smiled.

"I hope Taylor and the rest of your people return safely. If you're right, we'll need them more than ever in the coming days and months."

White patted Kelly on the shoulder and carried on down the hallway where the crowd was beginning to thin out. He stopped in a quiet spot and leaned against the wall and exhaled sharply. He should have known he would make no progress there, but he'd had to try. The General leaned back further against the wall and looked up to the bright lights running the length of the hallway. He was thinking of Taylor and the rest that he had left behind. He prayed they had come to no harm. He looked back down and was about to stand up straight again when a voice rang out next to him.

"Your boy Taylor is in the shit now. I hope he gets what is coming to him."

White was still fuming from the insults and stupidity he had witnessed and received before the President's eyes. He looked to his side and saw it was Dupont strolling past with his aide. His anger overcame him, and he leapt off from the wall and thrust a hard punch into the Frenchman's ribs. Dupont's body folded at his waist from the pain as he let out a squirm in pain.m The Brigadier's aide froze and watched in shock and disbelief at the scene. He would not go Dupont's aid, for it would mean striking a General. White looked to the frightened Lieutenant.

"How do you live with it, with a wretch like this? He isn't worthy of your nation's uniform."

White grabbed the scuff of Dupont's shirt and wrenched him upwards, hauling him in close.

"You're scum. Disloyal, jealous, greedy, self-centred and zealous; everything I hate in a man. Were you a marine, I'd have you shot, and I'd probably do it myself. You hate Major Taylor because you are a coward, and he is a hero. One of thousands of heroes I know. Thousands who may die out there while weasels like you sit back in comfort. One day, Taylor is going to come for you, and I won't be the one to stop him."

He struck him with a quick jab to the same bruised rib once again and tossed him against the wall. The General strode away in disgust, but if he was honest to himself, it felt good to deal out a little pain.

It was a long time since he'd been a field officer, and it was men like Dupont who made him wish he'd stayed as one. As he reached a turn up ahead, he noticed Commander Kelly once again.

"You know, it's incidents like that which have put Taylor behind bars more than once," he said with a smile.

"Yeah, and now I can understand why it's worth it."

"Dupont is a bastard, but he's also one of us. If we can't stand together in times like these, what chance do we have?"

"You'll get no argument from me."

The General continued onwards at a quick pace.

"Good luck to you, General, and may you bring our comrades back home."

It was only a few hours later when the General was once again setting off from Earth. He didn't want to leave familiar lands. He was reminded of how much Taylor had always voiced his hatred of space, and he knew exactly what he meant.

"Chart a course to the gateway, maximum speed."

* * *

"Sir, we've got reports back from our recon missions."

Huber looked up in the hope of good news. Taylor sat by him at the briefing table. There had been nothing more to discuss for the last hour, and it had largely passed staring at the screens.

"Go on, Captain."

Vega tapped a few buttons on the console before them and brought up a few images of an enemy fleet.

"The remnants of those who attacked us. They've rallied at a point near enough halfway between here and Red 1."

"That's no accident."

"No, Sir. Looks like they're repairing and redressing their ranks, same as us."

"And awaiting reinforcements," Taylor added.

"Almost certainly," replied Vega.

"Mmm," murmured Huber.

"Admiral, we could strike out at them while they are vulnerable. Otherwise, we are merely waiting for them to grow in number and become a sizeable threat. If we succeed in crushing them, we could even continue on to the planet. Worst case is we fall back to the gateway here."

"You know we cannot leave this gateway, Major," replied Huber.

"No, you can't, but some of us can. Give me enough ships to take them on, and we will crush them before they can recover."

"It'll take you ten hours to reach their position," replied Vega.

"We sure could do with keeping their number in check, Sir."

"Agreed, but we cannot risk too much in doing so, what do you think Captain?"

"The Washington must remain in position, Sir. It is the core of our defence. But neither can we send too few ships that they sustain heavy casualties in accomplishing the mission. The Major will need an overwhelming force to ensure a safe completion of the mission."

"Then you believe it to be the right course of action?"

"Hindsight will only tell, but I believe it to be the best course of action, Sir."

"Very well, Major, then you will take six frigates and the Trafalgar."

Taylor's eyebrows widened.

"We still need your marines to defend the Washington. You can take one company aboard the Deveron. Admiral Uxbridge will of course be in charge of the mission. You can brief him en route. I'll have the orders despatched and confirmed within the next thirty minutes."

Taylor was taken aback. He'd been fighting to have the Admiral push forwards ever since he had gotten there, and now his wish was coming true.

"Thank you, Sir!"

He saluted and turned to leave, but Huber interrupted him.

"Major!"

Taylor turned slowly and hoped it was not all too good to be true.

"Your mission is to destroy that fleet. It will be for Admiral Uxbridge to determine whether it is safe to continue to Red 1. The priority is the defence of this fleet. If you have a solid chance of reaching the planet safely then take it, but nothing more. You will follow my orders in this."

"Yes, Sir."

Taylor had broken more than his fair share of orders in the past, but he knew he couldn't break his word to Huber. He finally felt like they were getting somewhere, and he rushed out of the bridge with new life in his body. Jafar was waiting for him beside the other guards and had clearly been there without rest.

"Still here?"

"Always, that was my promise."

Taylor lifted his communicator.

"This is Taylor to Captain Jones. Have your Company assemble at the Deveron immediately. Full combat order. Captain Ryan, prepare your ship for departure."

"Sir, you sure about this?" asked Ryan suspiciously.

Taylor smiled. *The Captain is already becoming familiar with my antics.*

"Orders direct from Admiral Huber. We're heading out. Be ready to move ASAP."

Taylor signalled for Jafar to follow him as he leapt into a jogging pace. He could feel his heart rapidly thumping with excitement.

*Finally, I'm coming for you,* he thought, as images of Chandra passed through his mind. He felt new life in his bones at the realisation there might be a chance to save his friends yet.

# CHAPTER ELEVEN

Chandra paced along the battlements to be sure that the troops saw her face. A small pulse from an enemy scout smashed into the wall just two metres from her position. Two of the commandos near her flinched but not her. A second after the pulse landed, a gunshot rang out from their own lines.

"Got you, you bastard!" shouted out the sharpshooter.

The Colonel smiled as she passed him, but their joy was short lived. A massive explosion burst out ahead of their positions, causing the floor beneath them to shake and them all to duck down behind cover. Dust and debris blasted over their position and knocked anyone still standing onto their backs.

Chandra was the first to peer up over the battlements but was soon joined by Warren. All was silent for a moment as the dust settled, but then it came; the thunderous sound of an army of Mechs advancing through the breach. The almost continuous drone of their heavy footsteps was a fearful sound to even the most veteran among them.

Through the smoke ahead, they could see a wave of drones pushing forward ahead of the main force. She looked down across the line to see that the troops were readying their rifles along the makeshift battlements. She looked back to see that the first drone was in range and in her sights. She shouted her order as she looked down the length of her weapon.

"Fire!"

She squeezed the trigger before the sounds had even left her throat. The shot alone was enough to signal to the rest who quickly followed suit. The first volleys were carefully aimed shots that stopped a dozen drones before they could get off a single shot. The next wave passed right over them and met a similar fate after getting off just a few shots. The first pulses smashed into the defensive lines and were broken across the mix of enemy materials and the human shields.

Chandra was glad of the cover they had assembled. It allowed them to fight in relative safety. Another three-dozen drones came through the cloud of dust and despite getting off several shots, were smashed by the volley of fire. The hall went silent for a moment until they finally caught sight of the Mechs. They were packed in deep, as the breach was still small enough that they had to enter shoulder to shoulder.

"Knock the bastards down!" Chandra screamed.

She wasn't sure if any of the troops could hear her, but it instinctively came out anyway. The Mechs were amassed in such deep columns that she barely had to aim and resorted to bursts, despite the distance they were firing at. The hallway ahead was rapidly becoming a corridor of death. Smoking armour and blue blood scattered every metre of the floor within a few minutes.

In just ten minutes, the bodies of over a hundred Mechs and many more drones lay there, but there seemed no end in sight to the enemy attack. Chandra ducked back down into the barricade and looked back to see there was now a constant stream of troops reloading at the crates behind them.

Suarez was among them and appeared to be casually going about his job in a fashion she did not consider acceptable of any soldier, let alone one in combat.

"Lieutenant!"

He looked up in surprise as if he'd been caught doing something naughty, and froze.

"Get to the CP. I want to know the current condition of all sectors!"

"Wouldn't it be best for you to go?" he asked.

She glared at him with fiery eyes.

"Get me the fucking info, Lieutenant!"

She could see him mouth some curse as he rushed off

in a huff.

"Arsehole," she muttered to herself.

Pulses continued to light up the defences as they rushed overhead, and others smashed themselves over the line. She rose up once again to join in the action. She gasped as she realised the Mechs had gained ten metres of ground and were pouring in thick and fast. There seemed no breaking of their morale. Tsengal was alongside her and giving everything he had.

"What does it take to stop them!" she called to him.

"Death."

She wasn't sure if he was trying to be funny or not, but it brought a smile to her face as she turned back and continued to fire.

\* \* \*

"The Trafalgar will be in range in three minutes, Sir."

"Thank you, Lieutenant," replied Taylor.

He stood on the bridge of the Deveron with Jones and alongside Captain Ryan. The Deveron was the smallest ship in the group that had assembled to sally out against the recovering enemy forces. They kept close to the carrier and within the defensive perimeter of the frigates assigned to protect her.

"Feels good to stick it to them, doesn't it?" Taylor asked Ryan.

"Hell yes, Sir. About time, too."

"Let's not count our blessings just yet, gentlemen," Jones added.

"You can be one cynical bastard, you know that?"

Charlie looked to Mitch in surprise but could see it was a mere jest, though not a very funny one. They both remembered the dark times of misery he'd suffered through. His present state was of utter joy by comparison. He leaned in close to Taylor so that only the three of them could hear.

"What really are your intentions? Will you really stop here like Huber has ordered?"

"The Admiral was clear that we were to proceed to the planet if it is within our power."

"And if it is not? Will you go anyway?"

Taylor was torn between saving Chandra and the forces on Red 1, and risking the lives of just as many aboard the ships he had been given by the Admiral. He shrugged his shoulders.

"I guess we'll just have to wait and see."

"Sixty seconds until the Trafalgar has a firing solution."

They all went quiet and watched the display screen of the enemy fleet ahead. They had formed up to face the human fleet but maintained their position.

"Why aren't they going anywhere?" asked Ryan.

Jafar, who was stood quietly in the background, spoke up.

"Because they have been ordered to stay there and await reinforcement."

"So they'll just wait there to die?"

"No, they'll fight to win."

"Then we'll end them," replied Taylor.

An intercom channel opened on the tannoy above them.

"The is Admiral Uxbridge. All crews fire when ready. I want no survivors."

A few seconds later, the Trafalgar lit up like a firework display as its guns opened up in a fierce opening salvo. The Deveron was still a way out of range, but they continued on course with the carrier. Fighters rushed out from the Trafalgar's bays. It was an odd sensation to watch the enemy ships hold their ground against such a relentless attack, as if they awaited their death.

"How can they not run? What purpose does it serve to stay and die?" Ryan asked.

"It serves their masters' orders," replied Jafar.

"See, you think you have problems with authority?" Jones laughed.

The Washington's guns destroyed two of the enemy's larger ships in its opening fire. The ships were the size of the human frigates, and both displayed damage from their earlier engagement. There were just five smaller vessels and one of the frigate size left, as they descended upon them at speed.

"We have a solution, Sir," said the gunnery officer.

"Fire," replied Ryan in a sombre and monotone voice.

It was a bloody slaughter and far from the brave sally out they had expected. The fighters rushed in against the last enemy craft, like crows encircling the dead and dying of a battlefield. Even Taylor found no joy in the senseless slaughter. The Trafalgar's guns continued relentlessly until the last enemy ship was blasted into a thousand pieces. Just as the guns went silent, so did the bridge of the Deveron. They all stared morbidly at the smashed hulks of the enemy ships. In the overwhelming assault, the humans had not lost a single vessel.

"This is what they fight for, this is what is a victory to them? They want to kill us all and feel nothing for it?" asked Ryan.

He turned back to Jafar for answers.

"How can your people be so cold? How can they want such devastation?"

"Former people."

"But you were one of them, you fought for their goals?"

"That's enough!" yelled Taylor.

"No," replied Jafar.

Taylor looked up in surprise. It was the only time the alien had defied him, and it was in the most unusual of circumstances. Taylor thought he had to defend his newly found friends, but they didn't need it.

"I am not proud of my time in their armies. I will not

defend their actions."

Ryan relaxed as he could see there was no fight in Jafar.

"Sir, we have an incoming transmission from the Trafalgar?"

Ryan cleared his throat before replying.

"Put it on screen."

A video feed of Admiral Uxbridge was displayed aboard the Trafalgar.

"To the fleet, well done. The enemy is vanquished, and we are without injury. A perfect victory."

Taylor took his opportunity, leaping forward to address Uxbridge.

"Admiral, we have succeeded in our endeavours here. We have the opportunity to continue on to Red 1, as Admiral Huber recommended should we meet with success."

Uxbridge took in a deep breath as he thought it over. It was clear he had not intended to do as such.

"We will continue onwards, Major, until we can scan the area of the planet and assess the situation."

"Thank you, Sir."

"Recall all fighters. We continue on without delay. Uxbridge out."

Taylor sighed in relief.

*There is hope yet.*

* * *

"Colonel! We can't hold much longer!" Warren called out to her.

She looked up over the defences to see that despite the fact the Mechs were being cut down in vast numbers, they continued to advance. In places their dead were now two or three deep, but they would not stop.

"How can we fight such relentless enemies?" she whispered.

"We have to fall back, or we'll be overrun!"

She looked around to see dozens of Warren's troops lying dead behind the defences, and she knew the casualties would be as bad or worse further down the lines. They held the ground nearest the surface. She knew the docking bay lay just two floors down, and that it was the last place they could go where there was still a way out. They're backs would soon be against the wall.

"Alright, sound the retreat. Fall back to the docking bay entrance!"

She jumped off the wall and rushed to the CP to pass the word herself. Jafar was closely at her side, but Suarez was nowhere to be found. His platoon lay scattered along the defensive line and had quickly fallen under the command of Major Warren. She rushed through into the CP to find the five personnel frantically dealing with communications from all sectors.

"Pack it up. Our lines are falling, and we're falling back!"

Corporal Bradley turned in horror at her orders.

"What about our comms?"

"Grab what you can, and get a rifle in hand!"

They leapt into action, grabbing everything they could carry as she ushered them onwards.

"Come on! Go!"

They rushed out of the room to find troops flooding past them in a frenzied rush to retreat. Many fought on at their backs to cover their retreat. Chandra dreaded to think how many hundreds or thousands lay dead at their frontlines, but she feared more the realisation that they may be burying themselves into a hole they would never get out of.

* * *

Taylor had been waiting anxiously to see Red 1. Never before had he been so eager to see an enemy world. He knew they were just a couple of hours out now and prayed for good news. He and Jones had not left the bridge since the battle, and Jafar would not leave his Major either.

"Major, we've got a visual."

He nodded for the Captain to go ahead.

A projection flickered, and several gasps rang out as they realised what they were looking at. Taylor felt his stomach turn, when he realised over a hundred enemy vessels surrounded the planet. Transports were pouring down to the surface. He could see no signs of battle but knew it must still be ongoing beneath the surface. They all gazed open mouthed at the frightful sight for a minute when a transmission came in from Uxbridge.

"Admiral Uxbridge to all ships. Come around, full withdrawal!"

Ryan nodded to his crew to carry out the orders, for he could not bring himself to say the words and resign thousands of comrades to their fate on the enemy world.

*Fuck!* Taylor thought.

They had gotten so close. The planet was in sight, and yet there was no chance of getting through to Chandra. He could not believe they had made it so far only to turn back.

"We could still..." began Jones.

"It's over," cut in Taylor.

"We're just going to leave them there?"

Taylor did not reply.

"Major! This is Chandra we are talking about!"

Taylor turned quickly and grabbed Jones by the collar of his body armour and wrenched him in close.

"Don't think I don't want to, but it would be folly to throw our lives away. Do you think that is what she would want?"

"I know she wouldn't want to be left behind to the mercy of those bastards!"

Taylor shook his head.

"What would you have us do?"

He spun Jones around so that he was looking at the video feed of the planet and the enemy forces in orbit.

"Look at them! What can we do against that?"

Taylor could feel Jones go limp. His anger was replaced with sadness and desperation as he slumped against a console and lowered his head. They could see several dozen of the enemy ships engines fire up and pursue them. It was enough to pose a threat in itself, let alone the remainder of their fleet.

"The Colonel will do her duty, just as I expect every one of you to do so."

"So they'll die down there, and for what?" whispered Jones.

"Look at the time we have gained for Earth. We've smashed two fleets that were amassing. Destroyed much of their weapons research and development. We've held them in their own lands. Every day we gain for Earth could make a difference in what comes next."

"And you believe that? You believe we are making a difference?" asked Jones.

"You are," replied Jafar.

They all turned in surprise at hearing the alien's inception into the conversation. He stepped forward to continue.

"My people believed they were the most powerful beings in the universe. Every victory you gain weakens them. They are beginning to see they are not all powerful, and that they might not win this war. I saw it the day I joined you. Continue as you are, and you may well win the war yet."

The alien's words had a profound effect on Jones. It gave him hope and did the same for all of them there. For most of them, it was the most words they had ever heard the alien say, and yet they appeared words of wisdom. He continued on.

"The Colonel is a brave warrior, and I can say I have been honoured to fight alongside her. Even now, in the face of armies so vastly larger, she battles on. She should be an example to us all."

The bridge fell silent once again as they reflected on his sentiment. The sights they had seen were dire, but he gave them all hope and the desire to fight on with a new sense of pride and belief in themselves. Taylor looked into the eyes of his alien friend and nodded in gratitude.

* * *

Warren's commandos were formed up at the next line of defences that lay at the entrance to the docking bay. It was a relatively narrow corridor and would only allow the Mechs to advance fifteen wide and without cover. The ramp they had to descend before reaching flat ground meant that few could fire on the human defences at any one time.

Troops continued to flood into the docking bay, as others

tossed anything they could find onto the makeshift wall. Many had left their shields behind in the frenzied retreat. They waited now for the enemy to reach them. Chandra turned to look across the hall to the other two entrances that were guarded by Klimenko and Chen's Battalions. They looked even more decimated than Warren's forces.

They had less than half of the troops they had when the battle begun, fifteen hundred dead or dying. It was a level of brutal devastation they had not known since the war in France. She turned to see Warren was reloading his rifle at the frontline of the defence. He looked exhausted, and his helmet had taken a glancing strike by a pulse that had burnt into his visor. Chandra strolled up to the Major, and he looked up to her as she approached.

"There's no leaving this world, is there?" he asked.

She shook her head.

"If this is to be our fate, let us make them pay a bitter price for it."

She smiled in return. The courage and resolve of all those around her was a marvel to behold.

"Here they come!" a voice cried out.

She took up position beside Warren, and each lifted their rifle into place.

"Come on, you bastards!" screamed one of the commandos.

The clatter of the Mechs' heavy footsteps roared up ahead and echoed from all the walls.

"Fire at will!" she shouted.

The first dozen of the enemy were cut down instantly. The next wave stepped over them and fired their cannons as they advanced. Several smashed into the mound of the defences in front of the Colonel, and she felt the wall rock and the heat rush through. She quickly adjusted her aim and fired two bursts into the faceplate of the first target she acquired.

She kept firing until her magazine was empty, leaping back to let another take her place as she reloaded. She looked at the supply crates that had been stacked for them. Most had their lids ripped off and were now empty. She looked to Warren who was thinking the same thing. Ammunition was being spent at a rapid rate.

"How much longer can we keep this up?" he asked her.

"We'll fight to the very last bullet, then we'll fight in hand-to-hand. I'll fight with my bare hands before I lay down and die."

"I fear that time may come."

She slammed in a fresh magazine and jumped back onto the defences to keep up the fight. There were plenty more of Warren's commandos who could have filled the gap, but she wanted blood.

The volleys from the humans were so rapid that it was hard to differentiate one shot from another. It was a continuous roar of gunfire that would have stopped any human army dead, but the Mechs never stopped.

They never seemed to grow tired, scared or demoralised. Chandra personally killed another four before retiring once more to finally let someone take her position.

She looked around for Tsengal, but he was nowhere to be seen. Then out from a side room, he strode in with a massive heavy weapon of enemy origins. It was slung over his shoulders, and she could tell he was struggling with the weight. He was stronger than any of them, even with their exo suits, which meant it must have weighed a tonne.

"You know how to use that thing?" she asked.

"We'll see."

He rushed forward, and two of the commandos quickly shifted out of his way to let him slam the vast weapon up onto the wall. The only time she had seen such weapons was mounted atop the enemy's armoured vehicles.

*I never thought I'd be pleased to see one again.*

Tsengal lifted it up to sight in the enemy before firing. The corridor flashed so bright it almost blinded many of them, and massive pulses rushed down at the enemy positions. The first hit smashed into a Mech that disappeared in a huge flash that blasted three others out to the sidewalls.

"Jesus Christ!" yelled Warren.

He fired again and every few seconds. The cannon stopped the enemy advance in its tracks, but after twenty shots the barrel was red hot, and Tsengal threw it aside. That was clearly all they would get from it. The barrage of the weapon had brutalised the enemy advance, but still they came. From just twenty metres behind them, Chandra heard engines firing up. She turned to see one of the drop ships was preparing to take off.

"What the hell?"

She stared closer and zoomed in with the targeter on her helmet to see Suarez sat in the pilot's seat.

"No!"

Before her cry had ended, the docking doors began to crank open. She rushed towards the small ship, waving her arms and screaming.

"Stop! You'll kill us all!"

The Lieutenant turned and looked at her. He could not hear what she was saying, but they both knew he understood. He looked down on her with disgust and felt no shame for what he was about to do. She stopped and stared in astonishment. In that moment, she felt half of the life in her body drain. She stood beside an alien who was giving everything to fight for them, and now she was looking at one of her own that was going to throw it all away.

Chandra lifted her rifle to shoot the traitorous dog, but she could not do it, and it was too late anyway. She turned to see that the docking doors were already half open. The ship's engines fired up, and it roared towards the doors. She lowered her rifle and watched in despair.

As the ship reached the doors, it burst into flames. A

pulse from an enemy ship tore through the craft and burst out the body into the docking bay area, smashing it into the ground.

"Incoming!" she screamed desperately.

Before the wreck had even hit the floor, an enemy ship burst through the opening. She opened fire and was quickly joined by a hundred others. Fire ripped into the ship that was a whisker larger than the ship Suarez had tried to escape in. The frenzy of fire smashed into the nose of the small vessel, ripping it to pieces.

The enemy ship had got halfway between the dock doors and Chandra's position when one of the engines burst into flames, and it spun out of control. Veering off course, it plummeted into the firewall of the docking bay, but it did not stop. The burning wreck smashed through the relatively thin wall and kept going. Chandra turned to Tsengal and Warren in surprise. None of them had any idea there were further rooms where it had vanished.

She rushed to the fallen wall at a sprinting pace and stopped to see that it was not a wall but in fact, a hidden entrance to a broad ramp fifty metres wide. The wreckage of the craft partially blocked the descent, and a survivor prized one of the doors off. She stood in astonishment.

The hatch burst off the ship, and a creature staggered out. Before it had gotten two steps clear, she riddled it with ten shots from her rifle. Warren arrived at her side with his rifle at the ready.

"Get everyone inside," she whispered.

"We have no idea where it leads."

"Doesn't matter."

She pointed to the open docking bay doors that were now forced open by the wreckage of Suarez's ship.

"Any minute the whole God damn Krycenaean army is coming through there. If we stay here, we're done for. Get them inside!"

He rushed back to his troops and sent runners to the other two Battalions. They'd made it halfway across the docking floor when a dozen enemy ships burst through the entrance with their guns blazing. Few stopped their dash for the ramp, and in the rush, hundreds were killed by the relentless enemy assault.

Chandra stopped inside the vast doorway and watched the retreat with her rifle at the ready to cover the remaining troops. Mechs poured over the defensive wall they had previously fought over. She took careful aim and killed one that toppled out over the wall.

The strafing runs of the enemy craft as they approached were devastating to the fleeing troops in the open. She watched wide-eyed as many more were killed instantly. Their armour was unable to stand up to the heavy weapons. Klimenko was the last man through into the ramp, having covered his troops as best he could.

"This is the end for us, isn't it, Colonel?"

"If it is, then we're going down fighting!"

"Is there any other way?"

They turned and rushed down the ramp after the last of the survivors. They could count their numbers in the hundreds. A bitter count after the thousands they had begun the defence with. They descended thirty metres before taking a full turn and continuing another thirty, and then the same again.

*"Where the hell does this go?"* she asked herself.

They eventually reached flat ground where the hall opened out into a vast room. Two hundred of the troops had taken up positions around crates, tables and wheeled vehicles. She stopped and stared out at the vast chasm. A chill ran down her spine as she recognised everything around her, thousands upon thousands of incubation chambers, just as they had seen during the first war. All were full of humans, as they had first seen them in Paris.

"My God!"

Most of the troops had been oblivious to the chambers as they had never seen them before, nor cared with the enemy hot on their heels.

"What the hell is this?" asked Warren.

"Your guess is as good as mine, but I can tell you I have seen it before. The last time we found these chambers with bodies still inside, it cost us a city. Ramstein. The enemy bombed it into oblivion to hide whatever secrets lay within."

She turned to Tsengal.

"Have you ever seen these before?"

"No, we have been asked several times, but never."

The alien strolled up to the chambers and peered into them with curiosity and disbelief.

"They'll be on us soon, Colonel. What are your orders?" Warren asked.

She looked around one last time and snapped out of her daydream.

"Keep moving! Whatever this place is, they clearly have worked hard to protect it. The further we get inside, the better protected we are from their fire. Who knows? We may even find a way out!"

"You heard the lady. Keep moving!" Warren shouted.

They beat a hasty retreat along the seemingly endless line of incubation chambers. Tsengal seemed to study everyone they passed. After five minutes at jogging speed, they came to a circular chamber that appeared to be the heart and core of the facility. Substantial dividers ran around the area. They could already tell they would make perfect defensive lines along the firing line they had just run.

"Take up positions here!" Chandra ordered.

She guessed their number at little more than three hundred now, and all huddling in tight behind the only cover they could get. They were only thankful the enemy would refrain from the use of heavier weapons, due to the value of everything around them. Chandra paced around the inner desks and consoles of their new position with Tsengal just as curiously striding beside her.

"We've never answered any questions about these things. Never have any survived long enough for our experts to analyse them. All they have ever had are first hand accounts by soldiers, and what good is that to a scientist?"

She could see that Tsengal was carefully studying much of the text and tapped several keys on a console.

"You understand what all this is?"

"No, not yet, but I understand the language."

She stood silently and patiently awaiting more information. Many of the troops were reloading magazines. Others watched the two of them intently. Tsengal didn't speak. Finally, she could not take it any longer.

"Are they clones, or prisoners or what?"

"I can't say. But they're being programmed."

"For what?"

"To live on Earth, but with programmed triggers and purposes."

"What?"

Her face turned to fear when it was beginning to make sense.

"They're infiltrating our society. Fighting us from within."

"It would appear so. It has not been the Krycenaean way to my knowledge, but no race has presented such a threat in our history as the humans."

"We need to get word to the fleet. They must know this information!"

Tsengal nodded. Warren had been listening in, just as almost all around had been. He stood up and paced towards them.

"How on Earth can we get a message out now?"

"We have to. The lives of all of us mean nothing compared to the value of this information."

She looked past the Major to see the grim faces of those beyond. They all knew they were reaching their end.

"I agree, but how?"

She looked up to the roof in despair and then to all those around them. She stopped as her eyes met Tsengal. He stood out above them all.

"You could do it. You are the only one among us who has a chance of getting out of here. Leave behind all trace of your association with us and rejoin your people. Find a way to get this information to Taylor."

"Colonel, I cannot leave you."

"You can. I am ordering you. Your death here will mean nothing. Worse still, our deaths will mean nothing if you do not do this. Promise me you will reach Taylor with this information."

She could see the loss in his eyes, and it warmed her heart to see such human emotion within him. He looked to the others he had fought so hard beside. Many nodded in agreement for him to do as she asked. It hurt him deeply to live on and leave them, but he could see they wanted nothing else.

"I promise you I will do so."

# CHAPTER TWELVE

"We've got visual, Sir!"

Huber spun around.

"How many?"

There was a silence as they all waiting with baited breath. Taylor strode up to the console of the man who had notified them. He had not left the bridge of the Washington since returning from their successful but deeply saddening mission.

"I've got twelve confirmed, no, more, many more."

The officer brought up a video feed display of the incoming forces. They were spreading out rapidly, and he could count fifty ships already and many more advancing.

"Christ!"

He turned back to Taylor.

"This is why we stayed at the damn gateway!"

It wasn't much of a consolation to the Major, so he just

nodded in agreement.

"How long until they are in range?" Huber asked.

"At their speed, ten minutes or less, Sir."

"Ready all weapons! Launch fighters!"

"Here we go again," muttered Taylor.

Huber stepped back and grabbed him by his breastplate and onto his feet.

"You better get your head in the game, Major. There's a war to fight."

Taylor took in a deep breath and regained his composure. Despite the vast enemy descending on them, he couldn't help but think of Chandra. The enemy horde closed the distance quickly and was firing in no time at all. Taylor had become so desensitised to the brutal enemy assaults that he simply stood and watched, as if he were sat at the movies.

*They're never going to give up, are they?* Taylor whispered to himself.

The Washington's guns opened fire as their fighters soared towards the enemy fleet. The aliens were closing the distance as quickly as they could, as they had in every previous engagement. Only thing this time, the human fleet did not have the firepower to stop them in their tracks. One of the destroyers to their starboard side burst open as a heavy pulse smashed through its bow and down the length of the hull.

Six of the enemy ships were destroyed as they advanced

and many more damaged, but it was not enough. Huber could see the enemy was about to burst through their frontline and cut in between the fleet.

"Major, prepare your marines to repel borders."

They all knew that a boarding action was now inevitable.

"Sir, we can't hold against these numbers," Taylor whispered in response.

"We don't know that, Major. Now man your stations and defend this ship!"

A few seconds later, their communication links with the rest of the fleet blacked out once again, in what was becoming an annoyingly familiar situation for the Navy crews. The bridge was reduced to fixed video feeds on the hull of the ship only. Huber watched in horror as several of the frigates ahead of them were smashed by continuous enemy fire and reduced to derelict hulks, with no life on board. Taylor rushed to the door where Eli's platoon was waiting for him.

"Pass the word. We've got incoming."

"We've got a breach!"

Taylor heard the cry from the bridge, and it was shortly followed by Huber's booming voice.

"Major!"

He rushed back inside.

"Floor five, sector E, breach."

"Any idea on their strength?"

Huber looked to his crew.

"All I can say is it's twice the size of the ship that breached us at the gateway, Sir."

"Christ," replied Huber.

"Sir, this is only going to get worse. We can't hold like this. We risk losing the entire fleet."

"You just deal with the breach, Major, and make sure all your units stay near to comms stations. This is only the beginning."

"Jackson's Company is nearest, have him informed immediately!"

Taylor rushed out of the door, without a word to Jafar and Parker. The platoon rushed after him, Parker at their head.

"Shouldn't you be staying on the bridge?" she asked.

"Probably, but we need to make sure this attack is stopped quickly before it has time to spread. Jackson will be heading from the stern. We'll head them off from the other side and make sure they cannot spread through the ship."

They rushed to the nearest elevators and poured in. Taylor already knew the battle was lost. They couldn't withstand such a brutal and overwhelming assault. Eli looked to his face and could already read it in his eyes.

"What are we still doing here?" she asked him.

"What do you mean?"

"You know we're fucked. Does the Admiral want to kill us all?"

"We came here to make a stand with the largest fleet in human history. Think what it would do to morale if we ran at first sight of an enemy fleet. We can't leave unless it is clear we can't win."

"So we'll throw lives away to prove a point?"

"That's about the sum of it," he replied.

"At least there is a point to these deaths. Krycenaean lords will throw you to your deaths without reason," said Jafar.

"And that is why we will win in the end, because we value our people," Taylor said quietly.

Jafar's reminder of how despicable the enemy was brought him a new sense of purpose. If he could not save Chandra, he would at least make their foes pay a wicked price. The elevator doors opened, and they rushed out at a fast jogging pace. They didn't have time to carefully check every corner. If they didn't stem the flow of the enemy advance, the ship would be infested.

Within a few minutes, they heard gunfire raging as the sounds of war echoed down the long broad corridors of the ship.

"We're close now," whispered Taylor.

A crossroads lay up ahead, but Taylor didn't slow down. He could hear the fighting long off down the right turn and rushed to it, taking the bend. He stopped dead as he came face to face with a column of Mechs who were advancing briskly towards him. They were just fifteen metres ahead. Parker took the bend soon after him and stopped with a gasp.

Taylor leapt back and threw Parker out of the corridor and himself the other way as the first pulses flashed ahead. He slammed back against the entrance to the hallway and took a deep breath to calm him, for his heart had almost stopped. He drew a grenade and tossed it down the corridor, without peering around the corner.

The blast rang out a few seconds later, and he was quick to bring his rifle to bear against the stunned and wounded creatures, but many more pushed forward. Parker joined him, firing from the other side of the archway. They both ducked back as a hail of pulses rushed towards them.

"Damn good timing!" Taylor grinned.

They both knew that if they'd been just a minute later, they'd likely not have contained the spread of the Mechs.

"Think this is the only breach?" Parker called out.

"I doubt it!"

* * *

The vast chasm of human incubators was eerily silent as they awaited the incoming hordes. The few hundred survivors had long accepted they were going to die. As they sat waiting for their time to come, all most could think was of their bitter hatred of the enemy.

Chandra sat with her back against one of the consoles,

looking out to the defensive line of troops formed up at the outer circle. The wall they defended was just a metre high, and enough to provide a little cover at least. Major Warren sat next to her with his rifle propped beside him.

"You really think he'll reach Taylor?" asked Warren.

"I can't say I was fond of Taylor bringing those two into our ranks, but they have proven themselves more than capable of the task. I'd put my life in their hands. If anyone can do it, it'll be him."

"Humanity has held together throughout this and that has kept us strong. If they can eat away at us from the inside with these things, it could be the end for us all."

"Then pray Tsengal makes it through."

A droning sound rang out of the continuous clatter of footsteps. She stood up to look out over their lines and could see columns of Mechs advancing towards them for as far as she could see. They would be in range within a minute. She looked down to see all the troops looking to her for a last few words before the end.

"Less than three thousand of us held this planet against a number many times that. They may finish us here, but not without paying a heavier price than us. We have single-handedly halted the advance of their troops. They're going for Earth again. I have no doubt about that. What have we done here? We've given them a reason to fear us. The human race will not lie down and die. We'll fight to the bitter end, and kill ten for every one of us that falls!"

She paced along the lines and could see little hope among the troops.

"When this war began, the enemy were a frightful sight to us all, but now we stand as Gods against them. Superior soldiers - superior people in every way. If this is our end, then I am proud to say I stand beside the best that ever was. Our deaths will not be in vain. We've bought valuable time for our people back home, and made these bastards pay dearly. Now let's make them bleed a little more!"

A cheer rang out as she rushed up to the line and lifted her rifle, firing a well-aimed burst at the first Mech her sights found. It dropped dead and was trampled underfoot by the next rank.

"Come on, you bastards!" she shouted.

The rest of the troops opened up with a devastating volley that decimated two full ranks of the enemy soldiers. Blue blood spewed out of the metal floor and the incubation chambers beside them. Glass shattered as shrapnel ripped into the rows, and human blood seeped out from the chambers. The Mechs opened fire, and pulses smashed into their small defences and past them. Several of the humans were struck with their opening volley.

Chandra could not tell the three Battalions apart any longer, for the survivors fought side by side as one. She took careful aim with every shot and used just two or three shots per target. It was the minimum needed to bring down the heavily armoured enemy.

"Ammunition isn't going well!" Warren called.

*It doesn't matter anymore,* whispered Chandra.

She didn't mean for anyone else to hear her muttering, but Warren did and had to smile. He had accepted death was now the only path and could only laugh so as not to cry. The volleys from the troops ripped the incoming Mechs apart so that there was an almost continuous stream of bodies from where they had first come into range.

Chandra ducked down behind cover to change her magazine and could see more than fifty of their own were dead or dying. Several more who were wounded continued to fight on. She looked down to see she had just two magazines left. Chandra slammed in one of them and jumped up to continue firing.

Despite the number of Mechs that continued to fall, they were still gaining ground. Within just a minute, her magazine was empty. She looked around to see that many others were running dry. She fired off her last magazine quickly and threw her rifle down. She drew out her Assegai, and several others could already see what was coming and followed suit. She leapt onto the small wall they had defended and thrust it into the air.

"Come on!" she screamed.

She turned and jumped to the ground beyond and was immediately at a running pace. Their shields were long gone, but the rest of the troops were hot on her heels. Several fired the last of the ammunition as they charged before drawing the last weapons they had. Pulses cut thirty of the humans down as they closed the distance, but Chandra made it at the front by nothing more than luck.

The Colonel leapt a metre into the air as she reached the enemy frontline and on top of the first Mech. She thrust the Assegai like a lance into the faceplate of the creature, killing it instantly. It smashed down to the ground with her still on top of it. Warren and the others were into action well before the creatures could respond to the Colonel.

In less than a minute, the area turned into a mass melee where every man fought for himself. Humans and aliens were scattered, and all fought savagely. Chandra ducked under the clumsy swing of one Mech, thrusting up into the next she encountered. Even with nothing more than hand weapons, they were still giving more than they got. But their numbers were too few.

As Chandra spun out of the way from one of the enemy's attack, she saw Warren shot point blank range with one of the pulse cannons. At the short range, the shot burst through his breastplate and killed him instantly. She was sad to see him fall. He had become a great friend. It only boiled her blood further, and she turned and screamed out as she jumped onto one of the Mechs, stabbing through its armour with three relentless thrusts.

Pulses continued to rip through their positions. Many of the oncoming Mechs fired into the melee, killing as many of their own as they did the humans. The bodies of both sides were amassing to the extent that Chandra now stood on a layer of bodies. She could no longer see or touch the floor. Soldiers from both sides dropped all around her. She thrust frantically at the nearest creature. As it dropped, all seemed to go silent.

She turned to the direction where the enemy had come from. The Mechs had come to a complete halt and were dividing to let someone through. She looked around in surprise as she stood in the line of fire of a hundred guns, and yet none fired. Only twenty-two of the humans still stood with her. Klimenko was close at her side. His helmet was smashed open, and his face covered in a mix of both his own and enemy blood.

Chandra pulled off her helmet. She could no longer bare the closeness of it. She stood upright and awaited what was pushing through the Mech lines.

"What is this?" asked Klimenko.

The all stayed frozen in place until the last line of Mechs divided and through the parting lines came the one alien she could recognise – Demiran. He wore a lavish version of the armour Tsengal had. It was adorned in alien text and gold. He looked just as Taylor had described Karadag.

Demiran walked with an eloquence and grace that the Mech armies never displayed. A black cloak hung from his shoulders, and a lavishly decorated pistol was held onto his thigh armour. He wore no helmet and bore a huge bladed weapon that was three metres long, resembling a glaive. The last metre of it was a broad curved blade, and the other end a solid metal ball with spikes protruding from it.

"Colonel Chandra," he stated.

"Demiran, you bastard!"

"Lord Demiran," he replied.

"I should have killed you when I had the chance."

The creature smiled wickedly as he lifted up the vast hafted weapon, inviting her forward and taunting her. Her anger overcame her, and she rushed towards the enemy leader at a sprinting pace. Klimenko and the other survivors remained still, watching in astonishment. As she approached, she used the power of her suit to launch her into the air, heading right for him, but to her surprise he was not clumsy and slow like the Mechs she had so recently despatched.

The alien Lord stepped aside and smashed the tail end of his glaive into her. It smashed her off course, and she tumbled down to the floor. She landed hard and rolled over several times until crashing into the legs of a Mech. It kicked her backwards, causing her to roll over again. Her body armour was all that had saved her from being crushed.

Despite her tumble, she nimbly got to her feet and held her weapon at the ready. She had underestimated Demiran, and she would not do so again. She circled around him with her Assegai held out in front. The alien had a grin on his face, and his teeth glinted between his wicked smirk. Demiran was enjoying it, and she wanted nothing more than to spoil his fun.

She rushed forward again, avoiding a thrust from the glaive, but was hit by a kick that pushed her back. Demiran rushed at her, swinging a mighty vertical strike that would have crushed her in one blow. Chandra leapt aside, and the blade smashed into the metal floor, cutting several centimetres into the thick surface.

As Chandra spun out to avoid the strike, she swung out with the Assegai, and the very tip of the weapon slashed Demiran's cheek. The burning hot blade scorched his flesh, and he stumbled with a scream. He regained his composure and came on guard once more to see the defiant Colonel was waiting for him. The smile was gone from his face. She was satisfied now.

Demiran charged at her in a frenzy, swinging the blade in a huge horizontal arc. She avoided the strike, but he used the weight of the blade to pendulum the weapon around his head and struck as hard a second time. She quickly lifted her weapon in time to meet his blade, but the mass and speed drove through it, cutting deeply into her armour and knocking her off her feet.

Chandra stumbled to get back up. Blood seeped through a gouge in her armour. It was clear to all that she was badly hurt. She lifted up her weapon to taunt the creature one last time.

"Taylor's going to kill you, just as he killed Karadag like the dog he was. You'll end this war steeped in the blood of your own people!"

He ran at Chandra, smashed her weapon out from her hands, and spun the blade around, thrusting the bottom spike through her breastplate. The immense force of the strike drove the weapon right through her and out the back of her armour. She dropped down to her knees. Blood poured out from her mouth.

Demiran ripped the weapon back out from her body. Blood gushed out as the blade was torn out from her chest. She didn't wince in pain, nor cry out. She moved back into a kneeling position and refused to lie down for her last few moments. She stared into the eyes of the alien leader with one last defiant glare, drew her last breath and died upright where she sat.

Klimenko gave out a booming battle cry and rushed forward with the last human survivors. They screamed with all the energy they had left as they ran onto the alien guns. They were cut down as they reached Chandra's body. Demiran stood and enjoyed the slaughter before him. But when it was over, and the last body dropped, he lifted his hand to his burnt and cut cheek, wincing from the pain. Chandra's body still sat upright where he had struck her down. His victory had been bittersweet and far from what he had imagined.

He looked out across the grounds they had fought over

and the mounds of bodies. A thousand Mechs had died in that room alone. Everywhere he looked were the steeped bodies of his own kind, with the so few humans that had remained in the last fight. The humans had always found the aliens to be relentless, but Demiran had learnt that humanity was not the weak race he believed them to be.

\* \* \*

Taylor threw his last grenade down the corridor and waited for the blast, then leapt out with his shield at his forefront. A pulse crashed over the shield, and he could feel fragments burn into the gaps of the armour on his right arm, but he kept driving forward. He was firing rapidly as he advanced with Jafar at his side. There were three Mechs left, and their hail of gunfire cut them down as they continued to advance.

The platoon didn't stop and passed through their vanquished foes before the last one had finally collapsed lifelessly to the deck. Taylor led them on and around another corner towards where the breach had originated. He caught sight of movement up ahead and raised his rifle to fire when he recognised the outline of one of their own. He lowered his rifle and rushed ahead to find they had reached Jackson's unit; the Captain was only a few men down the line. They were reloading their weapons and had clearly just finished off the remaining attackers.

"Good to see you, Major," he said when he saw Taylor approaching.

"Did you get them all?"

"Except a few that made their way to where you just came from."

"They're dealt with."

Taylor saw a comms module down the corridor and hurried to it to gain contact with the bridge.

"This is Major Taylor. Floor 5 breach is clear."

"Major, we've had three further breaches. Several enemy units remain unaccounted for throughout the ship," replied Huber.

"Is the bridge secure?"

"We have had no enemy contact as of yet. Hang on, Major."

The line went silent, and Taylor waited for the bad news. He knew it could not mean anything good.

"I lost a few dozen in this last fight. We haven't got the strength to cover all sectors, and with the enemy scattering in the ship, we'll be in trouble before long," Jackson said.

Taylor nodded in agreement.

"That's for sure. We stay here much longer, and we're all finished."

The comms channel crackled again.

"Major, we've got a breach on the floor above you, sector B."

"Affirmative, we're on it."

He turned to Jackson. "I need to reach the bridge."

"Go, we'll handle this."

"Good luck, Captain."

"And to you, Sir."

Taylor gestured for Jafar to follow with Parker's platoon in tow. They got to the elevators to find the bodies of five Navy personnel and no enemy in sight.

"This doesn't look good," whispered Parker.

Taylor continued on past and leapt into the elevator with the remainder of their force in the one next to them. As the doors began to close, Mitch just made out the shape of a Mech turning the bend ahead. He lifted his rifle and fired a quick burst as the doors were closing. They slammed shut, and the pulse smashed in, buckling the doors and burning through in several places.

Mitch smashed his fist down on the button for the bridge level and prayed it was still operational. To their relief the elevator screeched, the buckled doors scraped on the shaft, but the elevator continued onwards. He looked to Eli to see the relief in her eyes. They both knew that they were very lucky.

When they reached their floor, Taylor had his weapon raised at the ready. He half expected to find trouble the other side of the door, but it failed to open. The mechanism was jammed from where the enemy blast had smashed the doorway. He dropped his rifle so it rested on its sling and placed his right hand on the door. Taylor looked back to check Parker had her rifle ready for whatever lay beyond. She was already well prepared.

Taylor gave the door a hard tug, and the power of his suit ripped it aside, surprising them all. To their relief there was no sign of enemy beyond, only a surprised looking unit of Navy guards. Taylor kicked the other door aside and stepped out.

"Is the bridge clear?" he asked.

"Yes, Sir," one replied hesitantly.

"Come on!" he shouted to his unit.

They rushed on to the bridge and passed dozens of the sailors. They manned their positions, but he could see they were scared, more so than ever. If there were anywhere to run, he suspected they would have already done so. He rushed onto the bridge to find Huber frantically trying to re-route Ota's unit. He finished the message and turned to Taylor.

The Admiral's face was pale. He looked as if he'd aged five years in the process of the battle. He slumped down in a chair by his briefing table and looked at the display screens of the ongoing battle. Taylor stepped up to look at the same monitors and could see wrecks and damaged ships on every screen. Fighters still slugged it out, and the capitol ships pounded each other with their heavy guns.

"Sir, we can't hold out here any longer. If we don't leave now, we may never get home."

Huber didn't reply.

"Sir, we're losing the fleet!" yelled Taylor.

The room was silent, and everyone looked to the Major whose yell at the Admiral went unchallenged.

"We've given everything we have to give here, but we cannot win."

Huber looked up and nodded in agreement.

"It is a bitter end to our endeavour."

"It is."

Huber turned to his crew.

"Activate the jump gate, and begin our approach."

Nobody celebrated the news, although they were all glad to be leaving the fight behind. Taylor looked at the display screens again and could see that despite their heavy losses, they had inflicted just as much damage on the enemy fleet. Dozens of enemy ships floated in space as hulks. The bodies of both human and alien crews were scattered throughout the battleground where they had been blown clear of the vessels.

"Give me a damage report," whispered Huber.

He was so faint they barely heard him.

"Sir, we have damage on fifteen levels. Fifty percent of our guns are damaged or destroyed. Reports of dead on many levels and from alien forces still roaming the ship. It's a miracle our engines are still operable, Sir."

He nodded again. It was a morsel of good news amongst a mound of bad.

"Gateway is coming online, Sir."

"What's stopping the enemy fleet following us through?" asked Parker.

Taylor turned in surprise to see her there. He thought she'd remained outside with the rest of her platoon. Jafar had somehow pushed through onto the bridge also. No one had dared stop him.

"They will not follow," he said.

Huber looked up in surprise. He was about to speak but held his tongue as Jafar continued.

"Their purpose here is done. They need to repair and recover from this as much as we do."

"Indeed," replied Huber with a sigh. "The glorious Liberty Battlegroup, look at us now. Tail between our legs and almost crippled. All this loss of life, and for what?"

"We could not lie about on Earth and do nothing. We had to know what was out here. We had to try."

"Gateway is active, Sir!"

"Take us through!"

The engines fired up to full, and they could see the rest of the fleet was doing the same, but the enemy continued to bombard them with a ruthless assault. The crew of the bridge watched and prayed they'd make it through. As they reached the gateway entrance, they saw one of their frigates hit by several pulses, and its engines cut out. It was still moving forward, and they could only hope the momentum was enough to get them through the Gateway in time.

"Almost there. Come on," Parker whispered.

The Washington passed through the gateway entrance, but the crew said nothing as they waited to see their own solar system. Seconds later, they burst out into their own lands to a hail of cheers. Those present had survived, and it was worth celebrating.

"Monitor the gateway. As soon the whole fleet is through, then shut it down," Huber ordered.

"And if they don't all make it through?"

"They've got sixty seconds longer, and then you shut it down, Lieutenant."

Taylor turned to Parker.

"There must still be Mechs aboard. Spread the word. I want a clear sweep of the entire ship."

She nodded in return and went to the nearest communication console, only to realise that they now had normal comms back. She lifted the device and passed on Taylor's orders. The rest of the crew all watched the fleet passing through, but there was no sign of the crippled frigate. Vega turned to the Admiral for confirmation, but he only nodded for the Captain to shut down the gateway. The swirling gateway shut down, and all that was left was the circular hollow structure.

Huber slumped down with his head in his hands. As glad as they all were to have survived, it was a bitter defeat.

"We gave as good as we got," Taylor said.

"Yes, but that isn't enough," replied Huber in a muffled

manner. His hands partly covered his mouth. He suddenly looked up to the Major and directly into his eyes.

"Did we have an impact, or have we just condemned Earth to another great war?"

"The war never ended. Those bastards were always coming for us, no matter what. Maybe now those idiots at home will back us with what we need."

"Sir, we have an incoming transmission from General White. His ship is twenty kilometres out."

"Put him through."

A projection came up. The General looked aghast, and they could already tell he had seen the state of the fleet, which was halved in number and badly mauled.

"Admiral Huber, I am sorry to say that my petition had no effect. No one would supply troops for our endeavour."

"I am sure you did everything you could. But now they'll have no choice. The enemy is coming for us, whether they like it or not. We lost many valuable lives these past weeks, but not in vain. You're cleared to board, General."

White nodded, cutting out the transmission without another word. There was little else to say.

"We've got a hell of a fight coming."

"And finally we have taken them on in space and held our own," replied Taylor.

"Just about, but we'll need many more ships and crews if we're to make a difference the next time they come through that gateway."

The three sixty-degree viewing display came back online, showing the true extent of the damage to their fleet. Taylor stood in absolute astonishment at what he saw. He was amazed the Trafalgar had even made it through. Large parts of its hull had been torn off, and one of its engines was missing.

He thought back to Chandra. Although he had not been there to see it, he knew she was dead. No one could have survived the onslaught of the vast forces he had seen attacking the planet she held. It was deeply saddening to have lost such a good friend, but all he could now think was at least she could rest in peace.

For now they had a new hell to face.